ROSIE BROWN

A Game of Two Halves

by

STEPHEN DIGNALL

First edition: February 2024

Cover Design: Getcovers

Editor: Julie Guthrie - Say it Write (sayitwritegc@gmail.com)

Published by: McStay

McStay

Table of Contents

CHAPTER ONE

Mum breezed into the bedroom, threw open the curtains and shouted, 'Wakey wakey, rise and shine, time to get up!' Every morning it was the same old routine. I'd heard it so many times it was beginning to wear thin, but if it amused her then what the heck!

I've been at the St. Elfleda's convent school since I was seven—that's where I met my best friends, Bernie and Jan. Since then we'd become inseparable. As we were the smallest girls in our year, everyone called us 'the three little elves'.

We would even talk to each other in a language we'd invented, much to the exasperation of Sister Maria. Whenever she heard it, she would berate us, saying, 'If you silly little girls stopped talking gibberish then perhaps your English would improve. Now hurry along, your lesson starts in five minutes.'

I was... still am... a sporty person. I go to judo lessons twice a week and I am a member of the school's gymnastic and hockey teams. I enjoy the kind of life most girls of my age would envy—

large house in the country, private education, pony riding, holidays in the Caribbean.

I was increasingly aware how quickly I was growing up. Each time I looked at myself in the mirror, I saw my body gradually changing. My baby blonde hair was darkening and my freckles were beginning to fade.

I'd been pestering Mum for months to buy me a bra, but all she'd say was, 'You're not ready to start wearing one yet.'

While Mum was in my room stripping the bed, I said to her, 'I've just measured myself and I think I need a bra!'

'A bra would look stupid on you,' she said dismissively as she went about her chores.

I decided to continue pressing my case. 'Bernie wears a bra and she's the same age as me!'

'She's developing much faster than you are and obviously needs one,' she countered.

'I need one too,' I insisted.

Just as she was leaving the room, she casually said, 'Just enjoy your childhood while you can and don't be in such a rush to grow up.'

'I'd enjoy it even more if I had a bra!' I shouted, insolently, but by this time she was halfway down the stairs, my plea having fallen on deaf ears.

~~~

State school was something I was aware of but hoped I'd never encounter. Little did I know, this was the day when my life would change forever.

Unusually for me, I'd had a restless night and had awakened with an overwhelming feeling of foreboding.

'Your clean underwear and uniform are on the chair next to your bed,' called Mum. 'As soon as you're washed and dressed, I'll put your breakfast out. Do you want porridge or would you prefer cornflakes and toast?'

'I think I'll just have the toast today, Mum. Oh... and a glass of fresh orange juice as well.'

'I'd much prefer it if you had a nice bowl of porridge instead. A slice of toast's not going to keep you going till lunch!'

'Stop fussing, Mum. I'm not all that hungry and anyway, if I should happen to feel peckish, I can always have a banana.'

'Then I'll put an extra one in your lunchbox just in case.'

As I sat eating my breakfast, try as I might, I couldn't shake off this oppressive sense of dread. It was like a dark cloud hanging over me.

While Mum busied herself in the kitchen, Dad was upstairs getting ready for work. With hardly a minute to spare, he ate breakfast while fastening his cuff links and straightening his tie. He looked nervous, continually checking his Rolex. Grabbing his jacket and briefcase, he kissed Mum goodbye then lifted me into the air. There was a faraway look in his eyes as he whispered in my ear, 'Whatever happens, please don't think badly of me. Tell Mum I love her and I'm deeply ashamed of what I've done.'

As I gazed into his eyes, all I could see were two deep, dark pools of sadness. Wiping away a tear, he put me down and jumped into his car. He gave one final wave goodbye then disappeared down the lane in a cloud of dust.

Watching him leave, I had the uneasy feeling Dad was in serious trouble and was planning to do something desperate. What had he meant by what I've done? Expressing my fears to Mum, she soon dismissed them, saying, 'Dad's tired, that's all.'

Thinking back, I should have been more insistent. Maybe then things might have worked out differently, but when you're almost twelve you readily accept everything your parents tell you.

As the day wore on, my sense of unease intensified. I couldn't wait until it was time for Mum to take me home. During the journey, I was uncharacteristically silent. Normally, I'd be talking nineteen to the dozen. 'What's up, Rosie? Cat got your tongue?'

'Have you spoken to Dad today?' I enquired.

'Only at breakfast,' she replied.

'Do you ever ring him at work?' I continued.

'He's been under a lot of pressure lately, the last thing he wants is to have me mithering him while he's busy.'

'I understand that,' I said. 'It's just that... well... he seemed to be down in the dumps when he left this morning and I'm worried about him.'

'Once he's got things sorted at work, he'll soon be his old self again.'

When we arrived home, Mum busied herself preparing the evening meal while I went upstairs to change. She loved to cook and was proud of the fact she prepared a nice meal for us each evening. Dad was always home at six on the dot—you could set your watch by him. When he'd not arrived by seven, Mum started to get worried and immediately rang the office, but the phone just kept ringing out. She tried his mobile but there was no answer. In desperation, she decided it was time to contact the police. They didn't take much interest at first, taking a few scant details and suggesting he'd probably broken down en route and would soon return safe and sound in the back of a recovery vehicle.

'But if he had broken down, he'd have rung home by now,' she countered.

'Maybe he's stuck in a place where there's no phone signal,' the officer replied. 'If you can wait a little while longer, I'm certain he'll be in touch. If he hasn't made contact by the morning, call back and we'll send an officer round.'

Enduring yet another a fitful night, I checked the clock for the umpteenth time—five fifty-six. It was obvious there wasn't going to be anymore sleep for me. So, creeping downstairs for a drink, I was surprised to find Mum sitting at the kitchen table staring blankly into a cup of cold coffee. Dad was a creature of habit so not returning home without first letting us know was completely out of character.

'Morning Mum,' I said, trying to sound cheerful.

Almost falling off her stool, she cried out, 'Whoo... Rosie! You startled me. I must have nodded off.'

'Would you like another cup of coffee? This one's gone cold.'

'No thanks, sweetheart,' she replied.

She looked at the clock and said, 'Five past six. Do you think there's likely to be anybody in Dad's office at this time?'

'Bit too early, Mum. Though it's possible the caretaker might be in.'

More in hope than expectation, Mum said, 'I'll try calling them.'

'Can't do any harm,' I replied.

She tried several times until, at about half past seven, somebody finally answered. It was the caretaker. Mum explained who she was and he confirmed there was nobody in the office. Then, out of the blue, he confided, 'It's been panic stations here for the past few days. We've had the auditors in and the rumour is they've found some irregularities. I tried to find out what it was all about but everyone's being very tight lipped.'

'What do you think would be the best time for me to ring?' asked Mum.

'The office staff usually start arriving at about eight-thirty. If you phone at... let's say... eight forty-five, they should all be in by then.'

At precisely eight forty-five, Mum rang back. This time she was put straight through to the office. 'I'm Mrs Brown, John's wife, could you tell me if my husband's arrived yet?' There was a hushed silence and the background chatter instantly stopped. She felt certain the woman on the other end was holding her hand over the mouthpiece.

Following what seemed like an eternity, the woman returned to the phone and brusquely replied, 'Sorry, Mrs Brown but your husband's not arrived yet.' Then she said, coldly, 'We're very busy at the moment. I'll have to go now,' then slammed down the phone.

Convinced something was wrong, Mum immediately phoned the police.

By the time an officer arrived, Mum was out of her mind with worry. As soon as he sat down, she began blubbing and babbling incomprehensibly.

'Calm down, Mrs Brown,' said the officer. 'Take a deep breath and start again, this time slowly and from the beginning while I take some notes.'

Wiping her eyes, she began by telling him everything she knew from the time he left home up until the present.

'Does he have any financial worries?' he asked.

'Worries!' she exclaimed, 'he's a senior executive with Peterson-Lange and earns a good salary.'

Returning the notebook into his breast pocket, he stood up and said, 'Don't worry, Mrs Brown, people go missing every day. They usually return after a few days then start wondering what all the fuss was about.'

~~~

Hours turned into days and there was still no sign of Dad. It appeared he'd left his car at Warringsley Railway Station before taking the nine-twenty to Paddington. Using CCTV footage, police were able to trace his movements from Paddington to Euston. The final sighting was of him boarding the West Coast train to Glasgow.

There were vague reports of a man fitting his description seen walking in the Lake District. The witness had been particularly struck by the man's clothing, which he thought totally unsuitable for the conditions. But as there had been no other sightings, police dismissed this line of investigation.

'Why do you think he went to Glasgow, Mum?' I asked.

'I don't know, Rosie. Maybe he's had some kind of nervous breakdown.'

'Does he have any relatives in Glasgow?' I asked.

'Not to my knowledge,' replied Mum.

'Do you think that could have been him in the Lake District?'

'The police don't seem to think so.'

~~~

Awakened by the sound of someone banging at the door, Mum, wearing only her nightie and dressing gown, ran downstairs to see what the commotion was about. I stood listening at the top of the stairs.

With the security chain fastened, she slowly opened the door and, peeping through the gap, called out, 'Whoever you are, you'd better leave while you still can. I've already called the police and they're on their way.'

'Sorry to disturb you, Mrs Brown, but we're from the Serious Fraud Office and are here to investigate the misappropriation of funds from the accounts of Peterson-Lange.' Then, pushing a document through the gap in the door, they said, 'I've a warrant to search these premises.'

Reluctantly, she removed the chain and opened the door. 'My daughter, Rosie, is upstairs at the moment,' she said, nervously. 'Can you give us time to get washed and dressed?'

'No problem, Mrs Brown. We'll start by searching the outbuildings while you're getting ready. I'll need to place an officer at the foot of the stairs if that's okay with you.'

They searched the house from top to bottom, removing laptops, files and bank statements. And as if there wasn't enough to worry about, unpaid bills were dropping like confetti through the letterbox. When Mum contacted the bank, she was shocked to discover the account was overdrawn.

With our backs against the wall, and facing eviction, we soon hit rock bottom. But Mum, refusing to be beaten, managed to find work as a care assistant. And don't ask me how, but she was able to scrape together enough money for a deposit on an old, terraced house in town. It had been a real struggle but through it all Mum remained upbeat. 'As long as we've got a roof over our heads and there's food on the table, we'll be okay,' she said.

With St Elfleda's owed thousands of pounds in tuition fees and Mum struggling to make ends meet, it looked certain I'd be forced to leave St Elf's mid-term and start anew at another school.

Though we'd always known it had to happen eventually, the thought of never seeing Bernie and Jan again was tearing me apart. Mum could see how unhappy I was so, taking a risk, she applied to the school for a bursary to allow me to complete my education, and to our great surprise, it was granted. Now, I'd be able to stay with my friends till the end of term.

~~~

With our new home in desperate need of TLC, we rolled up our sleeves and set to work with paint and paper, begging and borrowing from friends and relations to furnish the house.

Mum had always been a home maker and with the aid of her trusty Singer, she worked miracles with old fabrics and remnants.

I'd successfully managed to hide our situation from my friends —until the afternoon Mum came to pick me up from school and instead of driving a Mercedes, she was now driving a Ford Fiesta.

Pointing at the car, Jan yelled, 'Isn't that your mum?'

'I can't quite tell from here,' I lied.

'I'm sure it is,' she continued, 'I'll give her a wave.'

Cringing with embarrassment, I didn't know where to put my face. That's when I had a brainwave. 'Oh, I forgot to tell you, our car's in for repairs this week. This must be the courtesy car.'

'Bit old for a courtesy car, isn't it?' sniffed Bernie.

'Must've been the only one available,' I retorted.

~~~

Mum seldom mentioned Dad. It felt like she was trying to erase him from her memory, but I couldn't stop thinking about him.

One Tuesday evening, having just finished my homework, I came downstairs to find Mum putting the finishing touches on some curtains. That's when I decided to pluck up the courage and ask her the question that had been niggling me for so long.

'Mum?'

'Yes, Rosie?'

'When Dad finally comes back, how's he going to know where to find us?'

'He can go to Timbuktu for all I care. If I ever see him again, it'll be too soon.' Then she carried on with her sewing.

She might not have wanted to see him again, but I certainly did. After all, he was my dad and no matter what he'd done, I still loved him and desperately missed him.

CHAPTER TWO

The first day of a new term and here I am, Rosie Brown, staring through the gates of hell—or should I say, the James Crawley Academy. For Mum it was just another day. 'Can't hang about,' she said, 'should've been at Mrs Jackson's five minutes ago, she'll still be in bed waiting for me to wash and dress her. I just hope she's not soiled herself.'

The mere thought of it sent shivers down my spine.

'How on earth they expect me to do all this and still have time to make her breakfast is anyone's guess. Anyway, enough of my problems.'

Giving me a peck on the cheek, she leaned across, opened the passenger door and said, 'Hope you have a nice day at your new school. I'll pick you up later.' I was then left standing, all alone in a sea of strangers. Mum hadn't been able to afford to buy me a new uniform. The one I was wearing had come from the school's uniform bank. I just hoped the previous owner didn't recognise it and embarrass me in front of the rest of the school.

They pushed past me as if I didn't exist, each one meandering their way towards an enormous building of concrete and glass. This was a far cry from the sandstone turrets and freshly mown lawns I'd left behind. A large man with unkempt hair, sporting the biggest walrus moustache I'd ever seen, was standing guard by the gates. He wore a plaid jacket and corduroy trousers and was attempting to bring some kind of order amidst the chaos. From beneath the curtain of hair covering his mouth, a rich melodious voice boomed out.

'O'Malley, stop fooling around and get into school at once!'

'Mason!'

'Yes, Mr Morgan?'

'Where's your tie?'

'In my pocket, sir.'

'It's no good in there, boyo, put it on. NOW!'

I must have looked lonely and lost because for some reason, he took pity on me, plucking me out of the melee and setting me aside. In a voice belying his stature, he said, 'You're new here, aren't you?'

'Yes,' I replied, sheepishly.

Realising I was ready to break out in a flood of tears, he whispered, 'If you want, you can wait here with me and once I've shut the gates, I'll take you to the office.'

Before I had time to thank him, he'd reverted to his default setting, coaxing and cajoling the stragglers to "get their skates on".

When he finally closed the gates, he said, 'Come, Blodwyn, let's not linger.'

'But my name's not Blodwyn!' I protested.

'Doesn't matter, stay close and follow me.'

Seeing I was still very nervous, he whispered, 'Don't worry, I won't bite!'

As we walked along, he asked me all about myself then confided he'd also felt lonely when he first arrived after leaving his home in Wales to take up a teaching position in England.

By the time we'd reached the office, I'd learned a lot, both about myself and Mr Morgan. In the doorway, a woman stood holding a clipboard as she impatiently checked her watch. Mr Morgan could see she was in a bad mood, so he said, 'Don't be hard on Rosie, blame me instead, it's my fault she's late.'

Completely blanking Mr Morgan, she looked at me and said, 'You must be Rosemary Brown, Mr Critchley's told me all about you. I'm Mrs Dean, head of humanities. No time to dilly-dally, come with me and I'll take you to assembly.'

Behind her back, Mr Morgan started pulling funny faces. How I managed to keep a straight face I'll never know. It was obvious these two had history and there was no love lost between them.

Nervously, I followed Mrs Dean as she strode briskly down the corridor until finally, we reached the hall. Pointing to some canvas and tubular steel chairs, she said, 'Sit here and wait; assembly's due to start in five minutes. When it's over, wait until your name's called then we'll assign you a form teacher.'

With a room full of empty chairs, for some reason I decided to sit next to a rather dishevelled looking girl with red hair and freckles. There was a pendulous dewdrop hanging from the end of her nose and she wore a crumpled, loosely draped tie around her neck.

Already I was starting to regret my spur of the moment decision to sit next to her so, not wanting to make eye contact, I focused my gaze on the parquet floor. But I soon found my eyes drawn to her podgy legs and heavily scuffed shoes. One sock was pulled up while the other languished idly round her ankle. There was a strange aura surrounding her—it was a smell I couldn't quite place. Though not unpleasant, it was somewhat unusual to say the least. Its nearest equivalent was the smell of the stale biscuits Gran used to keep in her larder. If I'd been more vigilant, she'd have been the last person I'd have chosen to sit next to. The chair felt cold against my legs. Tugging at my skirt, I managed to create a barrier between my thighs and the metal frame.

'Bloody cold these chairs, aren't they?' said, "Biscuits".

I didn't answer.

Holding out her hand, she said, 'I'm Millicent Hampson. My friends call me Milly. The rest call me "the ginger minger" but it doesn't bother me cos they're just stupid. What's your name?'

Once again, I didn't answer.

'What's wrong? Too stuck up to talk to me?'

Not wanting to offend, I said, 'I'm Rosemary Brown; my friends call me Rosie.'

'You don't half sound posh, where do you live?'

'Travis Street,' I grudgingly replied.

'Travis Street? Never heard of it!'

'It's one of the old streets in town. Where do you live?'

'Pine Avenue. It's on the Kingswood Estate,' she replied.

'What's your nickname?' asked Milly.

'Nickname? I haven't got one,' I replied.

'Everyone's got a nickname. If you haven't got one now, you soon will have, and it's usually not very flattering. But I wouldn't worry about it. Schtick by me kid and you'll be alright.'

With that, she sprawled back on her chair, legs splayed in an unflattering manner, skirt tucked between her thighs as she waited for the assembly to begin.

After sitting through one of the most boring twenty minutes of my life, the head finally asked everybody to "Put your hands together to welcome our new intake".

Following a muted round of applause, everybody trooped off to their respective classes, leaving the newbies to await our fate.

'See you later,' said Milly, cheerily.

Not if I can help it, I thought.

We were escorted by our year head, Mr Chamberlain, to Room 203, where registration was almost complete. Mr Chamberlain knocked, entered and whispered, 'Sorry to interrupt you, Mr Bolton, but I've got some new pupils for you.'

'Thank you, Mr Chamberlain. I'll take over now.'

Checking his list, he asked us if we'd like to introduce ourselves to the class. When it was my turn, I was quaking in my shoes. I was used to being in small classes of girls, but now I had to face a mixed class of at least thirty, all of whom were staring at me.

Awkward and self-conscious, I could feel my face beginning to flush up. To get through the ordeal as quickly as possible, I looked down at the floor and mumbled, 'I'm Rosie Brown and I'm twelve years old.' Then I desperately looked around the room for somewhere to hide. That's when I saw a face I recognised. It was big, round and freckly—it was Milly! She was sat by herself, looking straight at me. Wearing a huge smile, she gave me a friendly wave. Oh well, I thought, any old port in a storm. And without further instruction, I walked swiftly up the aisle and plonked myself next to her.

Whatever Mr Bolton's seating plans had been was anybody's guess. He appeared lost for words when he saw me sit next to

Milly, but I'd decided this was where I wanted to sit and he could see by the determined look on my face that there was no way I was going to budge. So he resigned himself to the situation and directed the others to their allotted places.

I soon settled into the school routine. It was larger and more impersonal than I'd been used to. Milly didn't seem to have any friends and chose to stick to me like glue, always trying to make me laugh by telling me stupid jokes.

Wednesday was PE. It was a lesson I'd been particularly looking forward to and I had brought my old school sports kit with me. Mum, having paid a lot for it, said, as it was still new, it'd be silly for me not to get my wear out of it. When we went into the changing room, everybody undressed and put on their leotards. Like the rest, I stripped down to my underwear. While I was wearing my old school's regulation vest and knickers, the rest of the girls were wearing modern crop tops and briefs.

I could feel them all looking at me and sniggering behind my back. My embarrassment was complete when one girl shouted, 'Oi, Bridget Jones, where did you get those big knickers from?' This was followed by hoots of laughter.

They were all wearing designer leotards, whereas mine was plain navy, embroidered with the St Elfleda's school emblem, bearing the motto: Alis volat propriis — she flies with her own wings!

'Take no notice,' said Milly, 'while they're making fun of you, they're leaving someone else alone.'

Miss Meadows called out, 'When you're ready, girls, follow me!'

Forming a line, we trailed behind her into the gym, where a low beam had been set up. Taking it in turns, she showed us how to mount the beam and maintain balance while walking along it.

I'll show them! If they think they can make fun of me, they're sadly mistaken, I fumed.

I'm not normally a show-off, but they'd made my blood boil with their silly jibes and sniggers, so I decided it was time to show them what I was made of.

When Miss Meadows shouted, 'Next', I pushed my way to the front.

Seeing I was new, she said, 'I've not seen you in my class before.'

'I've not been here long,' I replied.

'Have you ever done any gymnastics?'

'I've done a little bit,' I lied.

'Don't worry, when you're up on the beam, I'll be standing close by watching you.'

Still fuming, I strode purposely towards the apparatus, leaving Miss Meadows trailing in my wake.

Throwing my leg over the beam, I pulled myself up into a sitting position. Miss Meadows rushed forward, but before she had the chance to intervene, I was into my routine. It was a routine I'd tried previously but had never completed successfully.

With arms outstretched, I stood up.

Wobbling slightly, I made a half turn.

Placing my left foot on my right ankle, I adopted the arabesque position.

So far, so good, I thought.

Then I leaped into the air, landing in a low arabesque position.

Concentrate you idiot, you nearly came a cropper then!

Apart from the sound of the bar rattling as I performed my routine, you could have heard a pin drop.

No turning back now! I thought.

Taking a deep breath, I launched into the handstand position, made two pivot turns and did a cartwheel. This was followed by a straight jump and a split jump before terminating in an arabesque.

Almost over, I gasped.

Maintaining my balance, I took a deep breath then cartwheeled into a sideways handstand before finally dismounting with my hands held high in the air.

There was a hushed silence when I'd finished, then someone— probably Milly—started clapping... then everybody joined in.

'Where on earth did you learn to do all that?' exclaimed a stunned Miss Meadows.

'Just something I picked up at my old school,' I said nonchalantly.

~~~

After we'd showered, I accompanied Milly to the canteen for lunch. She was uncharacteristically quiet, having not spoken a word since my performance. We took our trays to an empty table and sat down. 'You were amazing in the gym today, you certainly put the other girls in their place. They'll think twice before they make fun of you again, especially that Geraldine Fallon.'

'Who's she?' I said,

'Everyone calls her "Jellybean". She's the one who walks about as if she's the queen bee. She's always showing off, especially in the gym, but your performance certainly put her nose out. I was standing next to her when you strutted your stuff, and you should have seen her face—it was a picture. She was absolutely furious. There was steam coming out of her ears. She thought she was the best gymnast in our year, then you came along to burst her bubble.'

'While I had the opportunity, I thought I'd have a bit of fun and wind her up a bit, so I said, "That's my friend Rosie up there, isn't she a brilliant gymnast?" She gave me one of her looks, then pulling her miserable face, she said, "She's just showing off."'

'Rosie, why don't you come round to my house this weekend and meet my mum? I've told her all about you and she can't wait to meet you.'

'I'll have to ask my mum first. If she says it's alright, then I'll get her to run me round.'

Friday afternoon was sports day. Mrs Braithwaite, who runs the hockey team, pulled me to one side and said, 'You're Rosie Brown, aren't you?'

'Yes,' I replied.

'I've heard you were in the hockey team at your old school, so I've pencilled you in to play hockey with me today. When you're ready, get changed and I'll see you on the pitch.'

'I'm sorry, Mrs Braithwaite, but I thought I'd do something different and try football instead with my friend Milly.'

'You don't mean that dreadful, Millicent Hampson, do you?'

'Yes, I do,' I said, 'why do you ask?'

She gave a sneering laugh and said, 'The girls who choose to play football on a Friday afternoon are usually the ones who aren't very good at sport. All they tend to do is run aimlessly round the field for an hour, shouting and screaming and generally messing about until it's home time. You're far too good for that.'

'Thanks for the offer, but I'd like to give it a try first to see how it goes.'

'Okay, you go and play football if you want, but you'll soon get fed up with that bunch of idlers.'

Mrs Braithwaite was right. There was no organisation whatsoever. Mr Preston, who was supposed to be supervising, took little or no interest in what the girls were doing. All he did was keep the occasional wary eye on us just to make sure we were behaving ourselves and not disappearing for a sly smoke or sneaking off early. Undeterred, I decided I'd watch the boys training to see if we could learn anything from them.

They'd set up a series of cones and were taking turns dribbling a football round them. I walked up to Mr Preston and said, 'Why can't we train alongside the boys?'

Looking down his nose, he said, sniffily, 'Who are you?'

'I'm Rosie Brown and I want to learn how to play football.'

'Be a good girl. Go and play with the other girls while I concentrate on the boys.'

To me, this was like waving a red rag at a bull. There was no way I was going to put up with this. I said to the waiting girls, 'Did you hear what Mr Preston just said?'

I might as well have been talking to the wall as they just stood and gawped at me. In an attempt to rally the troops, I shouted, 'Are we going to put up with this?'

Failing to elicit a response, I continued, 'We're not, are we?' They looked at me as if they'd just witnessed the coming of a new messiah. They could see how earnest I was so Milly decided to take up the baton, shouting, 'No we're not!'

'Do we want equality with the boys?' I continued.

'Yes we do!' they all roared. The wind of change was blowing, revolution was in the air.

'Okay, girls. Let's go and join them.'

A motley band of girls, led by yours truly, marched en masse onto the pitch to join the boys.

'Why don't you lot go and play among yourselves? You'll only get hurt here,' said their captain, Callum Jenkins.

With hands firmly on hips, my reluctant band of rebels gathered around me. Standing my ground, I said, 'You can't fob us off that easily. We might be girls but we've as much right to play football as you have.'

By the way Callum was glaring at me, I was half expecting him to punch me in the face. But seeing I wasn't about to back down, we just stood there eyeballing each other. That's when Mr Preston stepped in. Accepting defeat, he decided on a change of tack.

'Okay, girls. You win. You can train with us if you want, but I'll tell you now, it's not going to be easy. I'm a hard task master, and I don't suffer fools gladly. I expect you to work hard and be able to keep up with the rest. I don't tolerate slackers. If I think you're not pulling your weight, you're out!'

'That's unfair,' I protested, 'the boys have the advantage over us girls. Not only are they stronger, they've also been playing football far longer than we have.'

Mr Preston conceded the argument, saying, 'Point taken. Tell you what I'll do. I'll give you six weeks to get into shape. If by that time you've not shown significant improvement, I'll have no option but to kick you out of my group. Agreed?'

'Agreed,' I replied, keeping my fingers firmly crossed behind my back.

In a perverse way, I could understand his point of view. But I'd always been a stubborn child, so I was even more determined to show him exactly what we girls were capable of—even though my ragbag band of sisters appeared to be less than enthusiastic. Up until now, they'd been able to idle away their Friday afternoons just messing around, but through my own pig headedness, I'd managed to upset the apple cart. I could see they weren't very impressed with me, but I just wondered, when the six weeks were up, how many of them would stay the course. With this in mind, I decided direct action was required, so I posted a notice on the student notice board:

ATTENTION: YEAR SEVEN/EIGHT GIRLS!
I am in the process of organising a girls' football team.

If there is anybody interested in taking part, could you please add your names to the list (below) and join me on the football pitch any Friday at 1.00 pm. Signed: Rosie Brown.

I didn't know if this was going to work. But if only a handful of girls turned up, and most of the original group didn't drop out, we'd have enough girls to cobble together a football team. That'd be one in the eye for Mr Preston and his precious boys' team!

CHAPTER THREE

I kept my eye on the notice board and by the time Friday arrived, apart from Minnie Mouse, Olive Oyl and Penelope Pitstop, no other names had been added. As the deadline approached, my spirits slowly sank. With a heavy heart, I prepared to concede defeat. To make things worse, Sharon Murphy and Rhiannon Tate, who'd been the least enthusiastic of the team, were nowhere to be found. Now my team was reduced to seven. Totally deflated, we donned our football kit and ran out onto the field.

Forming a circle, I tried my best to raise their spirits. Although Mr Preston hadn't made it a precondition, I knew we needed to recruit more players. I realised that if we didn't increase our numbers, the whole idea of forming a girls' football team would be dead in the water. From the corner of my eye, I saw Mr Preston approaching with a determined look on his face. I readied myself for the "I told you so" but he patted me on the back and said, 'Well done, Rosie. Your notice worked.'

With a puzzled look on my face, I replied, 'What do you mean?'

'Over there,' he said, pointing to six figures kicking a football around in the distance.

He blew his whistle and waved to them. When they finally arrived, he said, 'Meet your new teammates!'

Two I knew, but the others were only vaguely familiar.

After introducing our new teammates, Mr Preston quickly put us through our paces.

'Can I have the girls on my right and the boys on my left please?' Then he made us follow the same routine as the boys. By the end, the girls were flat out on the grass, gasping for breath.

'Too hard for you, eh?' he said, mockingly.

'No,' I panted, not wanting to show him how exhausted we were.

Before we'd time to catch our collective breaths, he was clapping his hands and shouting, 'Okay, you've had a rest. Now I want everybody to split into four teams—blue, red, yellow, and green—and I'll select the captains.' He chose three boys as captains, then to my surprise, said, 'Rosie! I want you to captain the Reds. Now I want each captain to take turns picking their players. Rosie, you can have first choice. When the teams are picked, we'll start with blue versus red, followed by yellow versus green.'

I'd watched the boys playing and there were a few obvious choices, but the standout player was Callum Jenkins. He was quick and he could pass, dribble, and had a marksman's eye for the goal. So, as I had first choice, he was the obvious selection, much to the annoyance of the rest of the captains. To give them their due, the other captains seemed sympathetic to the girls and tried, as far as possible, to be inclusive. Once I'd chosen a striker and a goalkeeper, I started to bring the girls into my team. I'd felt bad not picking them earlier but if we were to stand any chance of beating the Blues, I realised it was what I needed to do.

Mr Preston had chosen me as captain for a purpose. He knew, as spokesman and ringleader, that it fell on my shoulders as to whether the girls were going to succeed. And I was determined not to fall into the trap he'd set for me.

The first game was a scrappy affair with not much football on show. Luckily, my ploy of picking a good striker and goalkeeper worked, and we won 1-0. The second game was even worse with the Greens managing to scramble a late goal.

We were now in the final. I kicked off and passed it back to Callum, who raced upfield. I sprinted to the left wing and shouted, 'To me, Callum!' I must have sounded convincing because he immediately crossed the ball to me then made a run into the goal area. Seeing Callum free, I ran towards the corner flag. Don't ask me how I found the strength or the accuracy, but I somehow managed to hoist the ball over the heads of the defenders and into the space where Callum was running. Trapping the ball with his chest, he dropped it to his feet, rounded the goalie, and slotted it into the net. Once we were in the lead, I marshalled the team to defend our goal, leaving Callum up front as the loan striker. We easily managed to hold onto our lead until Mr Preston blew the final whistle.

'You played well for a young 'un, Rosie,' said Mr Preston. 'Your positional play was spot on. You shouldn't have lied to me when you said you'd never played football before when it's patently obvious you have.'

'I wasn't lying!' I protested.

'Pull the other one,' he laughed.

Hurt by his accusation, I launched into a robust defence, declaring, 'I've played a lot of hockey and from what I can see, there isn't a great deal of difference between the two. You just have to know when to attack and when to defend, that's all there is to it!'

'You make it sound so simple,' he replied. 'Some people play football for years and never grasp the basics. From the very start, you looked in control, directing the play as if you'd been doing it all your life. From the little I've seen so far, I think you girls have the nucleus of a good football team.'

Then, uttering a word of caution, he said, 'It's not going to happen overnight. It's going to take hard work and dedication if you want to succeed.'

With his praise and words of caution ringing in my ears, we left the pitch tired but happy. During the game I'd been trying my best to encourage the girls while at the same time striving to impress Mr Preston. I think I probably succeeded on both scores!

~~~

The best way I could describe the next few weeks was hectic—but even that was an understatement. How I'd managed to settle into a strange school while adapting to my new home, along with the constant worry of Dad's whereabouts, I'll never know.

Regarding my new home, talk about traumatic. It was a nightmare! As soon as Mum took possession of the keys she couldn't wait to get inside and look around. Opening the door, she declared, 'Welcome to your new home!' That's when it hit me—the smell—it was indescribable!

With my eyes watering, I stepped into the dimly lit lobby and almost immediately stepped in something disgusting on the lino. Unable to keep my balance, I slipped and landed with a thud on the floor. Mum helped me to my feet and I angrily turned on her, saying, 'What on earth have you brought me to? It's a dump!'

'All it needs is a good clean and a lick of paint and we'll soon have a cosy little nest for ourselves,' she said enthusiastically.

'A lick of paint?,' I moaned. 'The whole place needs a bomb under it! Whatever possessed you to buy something like this?'

Suddenly, Mum who, throughout the upheaval had been my rock, burst into tears. Regretting my outburst, I put my arm around her and said, 'Sorry, Mum. I shouldn't have blown my top like that, especially after all the hard work you've put in trying to keep a roof over our heads. Tell you what, let's have a look around and see if we can figure out what needs to be done.'

There was wallpaper hanging off every wall, the paintwork was blistered and peeling, and there was mould and mildew everywhere. I suppose that's how Mum was able to buy it so cheap. The previous owners had left the place in a right mess. In the kitchen, the floor was a minefield of pee stains and dried-up dog dirt. A solitary stove stood stark against a half tiled wall, the top of which had vinyl paper peeling off it. The range was piled high with all manner of pots and pans, each encrusted with burnt food and mouse droppings.

The only appliance in the kitchen was a free-standing fridge-freezer with a faded 'I ❤ NY' magnet hanging limply from the door. It didn't bode well for its interior. Fully expecting the worst, I apprehensively opened the door, but to my surprise it wasn't as bad as I'd first thought. Its sole occupants were a curled sandwich, some mouldy cheese and a rancid carton of milk. In the sink, decaying food and unwashed dishes lay festering in dirty water.

What we discovered in the toilet, and for want of a better word, the bathroom, was best left to the imagination. I still shudder at the thought of kneeling on the quarry tiled floor and blindly groping around in the meter cupboard only to put my hand into something squishy and maggot ridden. Urgh!

Mum and I worked our socks off and, following countless bottles of bleach and numerous trips to the dump, finally managed to make the place habitable.

Mum couldn't afford new carpets so she hired an industrial carpet cleaner for the weekend. They weren't the trendiest of carpets—some were threadbare with holes in places, but Mum managed to get them looking like new. Where holes or stains remained, she'd simply put a rug or a piece of furniture over it. When all the decorating was complete and the rest of our furniture was in position, we had the whole place looking like a palace. All that remained were those finishing touches that make a house a home.

I'd told Mum all about Milly—how she'd befriended me and invited me round to her house. Mum decided that after all our hard work, we both deserved a treat. As she was particularly looking forward to meeting up with her oldest and dearest friend for a coffee and a little bit of retail therapy in Dutton, she decided to drop me off at Milly's house then drive into town.

Saturday soon arrived and as promised, Mum took me to Milly's house—a fairly modern, mid-terraced house. It was quite nice but looked a bit tired and neglected. I knocked on the door and Milly, who'd been patiently waiting, opened it. Waving goodbye to Mum, she took me through to the kitchen where her mum was busy with the washing.

'Mum, this is my best friend Rosie. You know, the girl I told you about!'

'It's all I ever hear—Rosie this, Rosie that, Rosie the other. You've certainly been a good influence on Milly, I've not seen her this happy in years. She's always hated school, but since you arrived she can't wait to go in. If only half the stories she's told me are true, then you've certainly been busy since you started.'

'They're all true, Mum!' exclaimed Milly. 'If you don't believe me, ask Rosie, she'll tell you so herself.'

Every space in the kitchen was piled high with clothes waiting to be sorted and washed. There were two large and two small feeding bowls on the floor and a litter tray behind the door.

'You can sit and watch telly in the lounge if you want,' said Milly's mum. 'Once I've sorted out the washing, I'll bring you both a butty and a drink.'

The living room was just as untidy as the kitchen. Milly's mum certainly wasn't as house proud as my mum. A dog lay stretched out on the sofa and the whole house smelt exactly like the biscuity smell I'd detected on Milly when we first met. Shooing the dog off the sofa, Milly said, 'Come on, Rufus, off the couch, you know you're not allowed on there.' Rufus, giving a dissenting groan, jumped off the couch and flopped on the hearth rug. 'You're not allowed there either. That's your bed over there,' berated Milly, pointing to a large dog basket in the corner. Reluctantly, Rufus, tail between his legs, slowly trooped off to his bed. 'Where are your sisters?' I asked.

'They're out playing,' replied Milly. Then, intriguingly, she said, 'I've got something hidden upstairs I think you're going to like. Hang on while I go and get it.' She disappeared then returned clutching something behind her back.

'Close your eyes. No peeping! Now you can open them.'

She handed me a brightly coloured box, which said: Highlights. Not knowing what it was or what it did, I continued reading: Temporary Colour Highlights. Six vibrant colours. Easy to wash out.

'Wow. These look fabulous. Have you tried them yet?'

'No, I only got the box a few days ago. My Uncle Sid gave them to me. He told me they'd fallen off the back of a lorry, but I've looked all over the box and I can't see any signs of damage, can you?'

'No, it looks fine to me. Maybe they didn't hit the ground very hard.'

'It's been difficult keeping it a secret, but I've somehow managed to keep it hidden from my sisters which, in this house, isn't easy. They're forever sneaking into my room and rooting through my things. How they've not managed to find it is nothing short of a miracle. I wanted to keep it a secret until you came round then we could play with it together.'

'It looks great,' I said. 'We're going to have loads of fun putting different coloured streaks into our hair.'

Two hours later, Mum arrived to pick me up. I didn't want her to see my hair so I borrowed one of Milly's beanies to wear. 'See you on Monday,' I said as I climbed into the car.

'Where did you get that hat from?' Mum asked,

'It's one of Milly's, we've been playing dressing up.'

'Not sure you should be wearing other people's hats. You never know, she might have nits.'

I hadn't thought of that. She was right of course. Even if she didn't have nits, one of her sisters could have. But it was too late now, the damage was done, so I kept the hat on all the way home. The mere thought of catching lice was making my scalp crawl and I was finding it hard to resist the urge to start scratching my head.

I helped Mum in with her shopping then took off my coat, but kept the hat firmly fixed to my head, waiting until she was safely out of the room before taking it off. I gave my head a good scratch, hoping that if the hat was infested, it would be enough to dislodge any remaining nits. Then I stood in front of the mirror to admire my multi-coloured streaks. That's when Mum walked in. 'What in God's name have you done to your lovely hair?' she cried.

'They're only streaks. They'll soon wash out.'

'I certainly hope so. I wondered why you were wearing that hat. When I looked in the rearview mirror, I noticed you were scratching your head. I think I'll have to comb your hair with a fine tooth comb then wash it in Hedrin before you go to bed.'

'Awe, Mum! Don't you think you're going a bit too far? They may be poor, but they're very clean.'

'Makes no odds. It's better to be safe than sorry. Don't want you bringing lice into this house and as for that hat, I'll throw it in the wash and you can give it her back on Monday!'

CHAPTER FOUR

Shannon Dunkley, Paige Logan and Stacey Walsh derived great pleasure bullying the weaker kids. And they'd singled out a quiet, baby-faced boy named Nathan Morris for special treatment. Every chance they got, they'd taunt him, calling him 'gay boy' or 'queer'. As I was smaller than them, I knew I'd be an obvious target, so as not to give them any reason to pick on me, I decided to give them a wide berth.

Ever since the Friday football matches, Callum had become friendly with me and Milly. Nothing flirty or anything like that, just stupid kids' stuff. He'd often come over to our table after lunch and sit talking to us, mostly about football. I didn't know much about the game, but he certainly did and he loved to talk about it. He seemed to like the idea that some of us girls were interested in playing football.

Whenever he stopped to chat to us, out of the corner of my eye I'd see Shannon giving us daggers. It was common knowledge Shannon had a crush on him, and it showed. Whether Callum was aware of it or not, I didn't know, but all I knew was that he enjoyed talking to us and we got on like a house on fire.

'Why don't we make a threesome and go watch United playing Mossop Town in the first round of the cup on Thursday night?' suggested Callum.

'I'm not sure my mum would like me going to a football match, especially at night,' I said.

'Neither would mine,' added Milly.

'My dad's going as well, so you'd be safe with us. He can pick you both up and drop you off again after the match.'

'I'll still need mum's permission,' I replied.

'If my mum knows I'm with you, she'll probably allow me to go,' chirped Milly excitedly.

'If both our mums say it's okay, we'd love to come with you,' I said.

'You'll need to wrap up warm. If you've got a red and white scarf, bring it with you.'

~~~

All decked out in red and white, I was ready and waiting when Callum's dad arrived outside our house. I couldn't wait to wave Mum goodbye and jump in the car with Callum, but Mum being Mum, she made me wait until Callum's dad knocked on the door and introduced himself.

'Hi, I'm Callum's dad, I've come to take Rosie and Milly to the footy match tonight with my son, Callum.'

She looked him up and down, then said, 'Are you sure it's safe for them to be out at this time of night?'

'Don't worry, Mrs Brown, I'll keep my eye on them and when the match is over, I'll make sure they're brought back home safe and sound.'

Mum carefully examined Callum's dad's car and made a mental note of his registration number before finally giving her approval. This was the first time we'd met, but on first impressions, I had to admit, I rather liked Callum's dad and thought him to be rather cool. Mum gave me a kiss, tucked my scarf in, pulled my woolly bob hat over my ears, and said, 'Okay, Rosie, you can go now but stay wrapped up. Have a good night and make sure you stay close to Callum's dad so you don't get lost in the crowd. I'll see you later.' Then, with a look of concern, she added, 'You will look after her, won't you, Mr Jenkins?'

'You can bet your life on it!'

With that, I climbed into the back with Callum then continued on to Milly's house.

United won 1-0 and, true to his word, Callum's dad brought us safely back home. I could see the curtains twitching as we approached.

I'd hardly time to get out of the car before Mum flung open the door.

'See you in school tomorrow,' I shouted as I waved them goodbye. I knew Mum would have been on pins all evening worrying about me. She'd never let me stay out this long on my own before.

'Callum's dad seems nice,' she said.

'Yes, he is. He bought us crisps and drinks at half time.'

'Why didn't you buy your own? You had enough money with you.'

'He didn't want us wandering around the ground on our own so he made us stay in our seats while he went for them.'

'Did you enjoy yourself?' she asked.

'Yes, it was smashing. If United are drawn at home in the next round, can I go again?'

'Only if you're invited and are accompanied by an adult.'

Taking that as a yes, I finished my drink and as it was now getting quite late, I made my way to bed. 'Goodnight, Mum,' I shouted.

'Goodnight, Rosie,' replied Mum with a yawn. 'Won't be long out of bed myself. I'm just going to tidy away the dishes, then I'll pop into your room to tuck you in.'

'Aw, Mum,' I protested, 'I'm not a baby.'

Secretly, I enjoyed being tucked in. As I lay in bed waiting, I began thinking about Dad. In fact, he was never far from my thoughts. I'd lie there most nights just wondering where he was, if he was safe and well, and most importantly, when he was going to return home.

'Mum?' I said.

'Yes,' she replied, anticipating my next question.

'Do you miss Dad?'

She didn't reply. Following a long pause, she finally said, 'Goodnight, Rosie' and silently closed the door behind her. She'd been deeply hurt and it showed. I could tell she found it difficult talking about him, but I knew deep down inside she was missing him. Sometimes at night I'd hear her crying in bed. All the bitterness and resentment was just her way of coping with the hurt and betrayal she felt. Beneath it all she still loved him and, when he finally did return home, she would probably take him back again.

~~~

The next morning, I walked into class only to be met by Callum, who was chanting, 'Here we go, here we, go here we go.'

'What a night we had last night,' he said.

'Yes. It was fantastic,' I replied, 'especially when we managed to score in the last five minutes. After that, Mossop threw everything at us. All I could do was bite my nails and pray for the final whistle. That was the longest five minutes I've ever known!'

'Yeah, the ref was well bent. I'm surprised he even allowed our goal.'

From the corner of my eye, I could see Sharon desperately trying to eavesdrop which, above the classroom chatter, must have been difficult. At best she'd only have been able to catch the few odd sentences. Her face was a picture, especially when she heard Callum raving about the great night we'd had. I'd been trying my best to avoid the three witches but now, through no fault of my own, it was looking inevitable our paths would cross. And from the look on Sharon's face, it was just a matter of when and where. I'd need to be on my guard!

Friday afternoon and we now had the nucleus of a girls' football team. We were rough around the edges but Mr Preston, true to his word, made us work just as hard as the boys. At the end of each session, he'd play the girls against the boys but was very strict on how hard the boys were allowed to tackle. Less so for the girls, which resulted in some dubious decisions being given against the boys. This usually ended in a hotly disputed win for the girls, much to their annoyance.

Monday morning and the school routine continued as before. There was now an atmosphere between us and the witches. We were often on the receiving end of some snide remarks whenever we encountered them, but that was to be expected. Other than that, there was no trouble and it was fully expected that things would blow over when they realised their remarks were like water off a duck's back. They'd turn their spitefulness onto easier targets—probably Nathan—but what happened next took me completely by surprise.

Our last lesson before lunch was Maths. When the bell sounded, we gathered up our belongings and headed for the canteen. As a rule, Milly and I would go to the locker room and put our bags away before lunch. The coven had been unusually quiet and appeared to be ignoring us as they hurriedly left class. Idly chatting, we meandered down the corridor and into what appeared to be an empty locker room. That's when we heard the door slam behind us. We looked round only to see the three witches blocking the exit.

Flanked by Paige and Stacey, Sharon snarled, 'So, if it isn't short arse and her lapdog, the ginger minger. I think it's time we had a little talk, don't you?'

'I decide what goes down in our class,' she continued, 'and I don't like the way you've been pushing your snooty nose into my business.'

'I don't know what you're getting at,' I said.

'You know exactly what I'm getting at! Worming your way into the football team just so you can be near Callum. Everyone knows me and Callum are an item, but since you came along he doesn't even look sideways at me anymore.'

'Nothing to do with me. He's a free agent, he can be friends with anyone he wants. I'm certainly not stopping him. And anyway, he's not my boyfriend if that's what you're getting at.'

'Don't tell lies, I know you went out with him last week.'

'Maybe I did, maybe I didn't,' I teased, knowing this would wind her up.

'I can't see as it's any of your business anyhow, so if you don't mind, we're both very hungry and want to go to the canteen.'

Taking the lead, I boldly proceeded to walk past them. I could see Milly was scared, so I whispered quietly, 'Stay close behind me, don't say a word and you'll be okay.'

We headed for the door, but they refused to budge.

'Could you move out of our way please?' I asked in a firm but polite voice. But they stood their ground, refusing to move. I decided to push my way past them and that's when Sharon made a grab for me. I'd been expecting them to try something and was well prepared. As soon as she lunged, I grabbed her arm and threw her over my shoulder, landing her face down on the floor. Still holding her wrist, I put my foot on her shoulder and began to twist her arm. The other two came at me, so I twisted her arm even further, making her squeal in agony.

'Come any closer and I'll pull her arm out of its socket,' I snarled, 'and don't think I can't.'

That was enough to stop them dead in their tracks. Then I said to Sharon, 'Tell your two goons to back off or else!'

She seemed reluctant at first, so I exerted a little more pressure and she screamed, 'She's going to break my arm, let them go!'

That seemed to do the trick. They quickly parted, leaving a gap for us, so I released her arm, dusted myself down and said, 'Let that be a lesson to you. But remember, this is only a sample of what I'm capable of, so if you're thinking of doing anything stupid, I'd think again. And if you ever start threatening me or any of my friends, you'll wish you'd never crossed paths with me. Comprende?'

They nodded. Then, using a mock upper class accent, I said, 'Come, Millicent, let us dispense with further discourse and leave these reprehensible creatures to their own devices. It's time we decamped to the restaurant to partake of their gastronomic delights.'

'I haven't a clue what you're talking about,' said Milly, 'but if you're ready for some scran, then so am I!'

Paige and Stacey helped Sharon to her feet while we pushed past.

'I think you've dislocated my shoulder,' wailed a sorry and dishevelled Sharon, whose grazed knees were poking through two large holes in her tights, leaving them wondering how their nasty little plan had gone so badly wrong.

During lunch I watched the threesome slink into the canteen, buy their meals, then take them to the furthest possible table away from us. 'Did you see them creeping in?' whispered Milly.

'Yes, I did.'

'Not so cocky now, are they?' gloated Milly.

'All I hope is they've learned their lesson, but knowing them, I somehow doubt it.'

Milly was unusually quiet for the rest of the meal. I could see something was bothering her.

'Penny for them,' I said.

'Penny for what?' asked Milly.

'Penny for your thoughts, of course. You've obviously got something on your mind.'

After a long pause, she said, 'Actually, Rosie... I was wondering...'

'If it's those three you're worrying about, then don't! They'll think twice before they try anything like that again.'

'No, it's nothing like that,' she replied.

There was another long pause, then she said, 'You know when Sharon began calling us names?'

'Yes.'

'Well, she called me your lapdog. Do you think I'm your lapdog?'

'If you're my lapdog then what are her two mates? I certainly don't think of you as my lapdog, so stop letting those nasty bitches get to you.'

Milly went quiet for a minute then said, 'But I do seem to follow you around quite a lot, don't I?'

'Not that I've noticed,' I replied, 'we're in the same class as each other and we've sat together ever since I started. In fact, if it wasn't for you, I wouldn't have any friends so like I said, ignore them, they're just jealous of us.'

Milly slouched over her plate, playing around with a random lettuce leaf. For her, eating salads was a recent innovation. Previously, she'd always eaten chips with everything.

'Rosie,' she said casually, 'don't you find you get a tiny bit hungry in the middle of the afternoon if you've only had salad for lunch?'

'You don't just have to eat salad, you can have chips as well, so long as they're not cooked in fat,' I replied.

'But you don't have chips with yours.'

'That's because I only have a small appetite,' I continued.

She gave a long sigh, took a deep breath and said, 'Do you think I'm fat?'

'How could you even suggest I'd think such a thing,' I said.

'Sorry, Rosie, it's just that you're so slim while I'm... well, you know what I am.'

'Yes, I do know what you are. You're the kindest, sweetest, most loyal friend a person could ever have. You always know when I'm feeling down and try to cheer me up with your silly jokes.'

With that she sat up, gave me one of her cheeky grins and said, 'I think I'll go and get a few chips on the side, that should keep me going till teatime.'

When she returned, she said, 'Do you want some of my chips? There's plenty.'

Not wanting to disappoint her, I said, 'Don't mind if I do.'

When we'd eaten, she said, 'You know those judo classes you go to?'

'Yes.'

'Do you think they'd let me join?'

'Of course they would, but you need to remember it's no good joining on a whim only to give it all up after a few weeks.'

'I wouldn't do that,' she replied.

Changing the subject, I said, 'You know what happened in the changing room before lunch?'

'Yes,' said Milly excitedly, then went on to describe in animated detail how I'd managed to single-handedly sort out three school bullies.

When she finally finished, I said quietly, 'Milly, I want you to promise me you'll never talk about what happened in the locker room again. I'm not supposed to use my judo skills outside the gym. If my instructor were ever to find out, I'd get into serious trouble.'

'I won't say a word. You can count on me; my lips are sealed. In your defence, the only thing I will say is that you had no other option but to defend yourself.'

'He wouldn't see it like that, he'd say I should've warned them beforehand and only used my judo skills as a last resort.'

50

'But you had no other alternative. There were three of them and they attacked you. All you did was defend yourself.'

'Makes no difference. The fact is I lost control. I should have warned them what would happen, but I didn't.'

'They'd have just laughed in your face.'

'Maybe they would have. But the two things you're taught in judo are: self-control and self-discipline, and I didn't use any of them. So let's forget about it and pretend it never happened.'

~~~

I'd briefly mentioned Nathan Morris. He was different. He stood out from the rest of the boys. He was small and thin with long hair and a pasty face. He didn't have any friends and rarely mixed with his schoolmates, tending to keep himself to himself. This resulted in him being picked on, especially by the three witches.

I felt sorry for him and tried my best to befriend him, much to Milly's annoyance. But even I had difficulty getting through to him, so in the end I gave up trying. With so much going on in my life, I allowed him to drop off my radar, but he was soon to reappear with a bang!

CHAPTER FIVE

Following the half term break, we arrived back in school totally unprepared for the bombshell about to explode in our faces. At the end of assembly, Mr Critchley, flanked by the rest of his staff, asked everybody to stay behind for a few minutes while he made an announcement. From the side of the stage walked a girl with a ponytail, who looked vaguely familiar.

'I'd like to introduce Natalie. You'll know her from last term as Nathan.' There was a gasp of shock from the assembled pupils. Milly whispered, 'Look. It's Nathan. Nathan Morris. You know... our Nathan Morris!'

'Could I have silence please?' shouted Mr Critchley. 'Natalie will continue her education in the same class as last term. I want everyone in school, and especially her classmates, to make her welcome. Natalie is starting on a long and difficult journey and will need all our help and support along the way. I wish to make it quite clear that the school fully supports her decision and we request that you all help her adjust to her new role in our school.'

'I have been in close contact with her parents and would like to stress that both myself and all staff will not countenance intolerance or bullying of any kind, no matter what form it takes. Anyone found to have been involved in this kind of behaviour, especially towards Natalie, will be severely dealt with. Assembly is over, please make your way to your classes in a quiet and orderly manner.'

Needless to say, the talk was of nothing else. Nobody had ever heard of this happening before and we were eager to see her when she finally arrived in our classroom. Mr Bolton walked in with Natalie and said, 'You've just heard what the head had to say. I'd just like to confirm that I fully concur with Mr Critchley and reiterate that I'm not prepared to tolerate bullying and intolerance of any kind in my classroom. I will come down hard on anyone who disobeys. Now, I'd like you to give a warm welcome to Natalie.'

It all went quiet and frankly, it felt a little bit awkward. Even Natalie looked uncomfortable as she stood in front of the class, eyes fixed firmly on her Mary Janes. Deciding it was time someone broke the silence, I began to clap, then gradually everyone else followed. 'Okay, Natalie, can you go and take your seat next to Geoffrey, please?'

Without making any eye contact, Natalie walked between the lines of children then sat down next to Geoffrey Wainwright, a nondescript geek of a boy with a spotty face and glasses.

Looking decidedly embarrassed, he started shuffling uneasily on his chair as he tried to distance himself from his new classmate. Mr Bolton, giving him a cold hard stare, said, 'Wainwright!'

'Yes sir,'

'Have you got fleas?'

'No, sir.'

'Then can you please sit still while we start the lesson?' This brought giggles from the rest of the class.

'The next person I hear laughing will be sent to Mr Critchley's office!'

Nobody thought it was ever going to be easy for Natalie. From relative obscurity she'd now become the biggest talking point the school had ever had. Although the pupils had to be careful what they said during school hours, outside school was a different matter.

When Mum picked me up, she asked the same question she always asks—What happened in school today?—expecting the usual evasive answer every twelve year old gives. But this time I did have something to tell her.

'Do you remember me telling you about Nathan Morris? He's the quiet boy in our class?' By the way she answered, I could tell she didn't.

'Er... Mmm... yes, I think so.'

'Well, you'll never guess what happened today.'

'I could sit here all day and still not guess, so don't keep me in suspense. What did happen?'

'It's so fantastic I don't know where to start.'

I could see her patience was wearing thin as she casually replied, 'Don't tell me, he had a sex change during the half term and returned to school wearing girls' clothes.'

'How on earth did you know that?' I said in amazement. 'Somebody must have told you!'

'What do you mean, somebody must have told me? You don't mean I am right!' said Mum, almost losing control of the car.

'Yes, it's true. When we went into the hall for assembly, the entire teaching staff was stood on the stage behind Mr Critchley, so we knew he had something important to tell us. That's when he told us about Natalie.'

'Who's Natalie?' asked my increasingly confused mum.

'That's what I'm trying to tell you.' Then I told her the whole story, finishing with, '...then he brought Nathan onto the stage and introduced her as Natalie!'

'You're making this up, aren't you?'

'Nope. It's all true. Cross my heart and hope to die.'

'And what happened next?'

'Nothing much. He... sorry... she came into our class, sat down and continued her lesson with the rest of us as if nothing had happened.'

For the remainder of the journey, Mum didn't say another word.

After tea, while we were sat watching the telly, Mum casually asked, 'What does Natalie do when she wants to go to the toilet?'

'Haven't thought about it. I should imagine she probably uses ours.'

She went quiet and didn't mention the subject again.

~~~

The next day, Mum dropped me off at the school gates and, as usual, I jumped out of the car, skipping light footed into school. By now, I'd got to know almost everyone in my year and except for the usual suspects, I was getting on well with them all. For some reason, I don't know why, something told me to look back. That's when I noticed Mum's car was parked outside the school gates. I looked about to see where she'd gone and saw a large group of parents had gathered. In among them I could see Mum. As I was about to enter the building, I took one last look and saw they were still there. Puzzled, I began to wonder what they could be talking about. It wouldn't be long before I found out.

I went to assembly, then to my class. In the meantime, the posse of parents had selected a spokesperson and marched up to the school. They strode into the secretary's office and demanded to see the head as a matter of urgency. 'I'm sorry, Mr Critchley's busy taking assembly, but if you're prepared to wait, he shouldn't be too long.'

So many people had crowded the office that there wasn't enough seats to accommodate them.

When Mr Critchley finally arrived, he was astounded to see such a large deputation. His secretary, Mrs Burrows, said, 'I'm sorry about this, Mr Critchley, but they were very insistent that they wanted to speak to you as a matter of urgency.'

'That's fine, Mrs Burrows, just let me straighten my desk then you can send them in.'

Mr Critchley had a shrewd idea why they were there, so he was able to prepare himself for the expected onslaught.

It seemed like an eternity before Mr Critchley's voice came crackling over the intercom, 'I'm ready to meet the parents now, can you bring them in please?'

Straightening her skirt, Mrs Burrows announced, 'If you'll kindly follow me.'

Trooping in behind her, they lined up in uneasy silence in front of Mr Critchley, who was seated behind his desk, hands clasped in front of his face as if in prayer. 'To what do I owe this pleasure?' he asked.

Mrs Mullally was the first to speak. She wasn't a particularly articulate person, but during the meeting at the gate, she proved herself to be the loudest and most persuasive of the group. And on that basis alone, she had been elected as the spokesperson.

She stepped forward and said, 'My daughter Tiffany's told me there's a pervert roaming round the school dressed in girls' clothes and hanging around the girls' toilets.'

The rest of the delegation mumbled in agreement.

'I really don't know what you're talking about, Mrs Mullally. We at the James Crawley Academy take school security very seriously. If anybody had breached our security, we'd have known about it long before now.'

He knew who she was referring to but was waiting for her to say exactly who she meant.

'It's that pervert you've got in the first year. Apparently he's decided to come to school dressed as a girl and has started using the girls' toilets and changing rooms.'

'If it's Natalie Morris you're talking about, then we're all fully aware of the situation. Natalie is going through a difficult period in her life and it is up to us—the staff, students and parents—to help her until she reaches an age when she's able to make the final decision as to whether she wants to make the transition.'

Mrs Mullally was now on a roll. 'I think the rest of the parents will back me up when I say we don't want that tranny hanging around the girls' toilets and changing rooms while our daughters are using them.'

A voice from the back shouted, 'Hear, hear! Three cheers for Mrs Mullally. Hip, hip hooray.' This was followed by a round of applause.

Mr Critchley waited until the commotion died down then, in a calm and measured voice, he said, 'I can fully understand that feelings are high at the moment, but this is an unusual situation and one we have never before encountered at the Academy. But the use of such emotive language is not going to help the situation. We have a duty of care to all the children, including Natalie, and we're trying our best to accommodate her needs and requirements. We're now in the process of organising separate toilet and changing facilities. And in answer to your fears, I can categorically state that Natalie does not, and never will, pose a threat to your children.' Before anybody had a chance to argue, he continued, 'I hope my answers have gone some way to ease your worries. I appreciate your coming to see me to express your concerns—concerns which I have taken onboard. I firmly believe the measures we are currently implementing are more than sufficient to allay your fears. Therefore, if there are no further questions, I'd like to draw this meeting to a close. I thank you all for your attendance.' He buzzed his secretary and resumed reading his correspondence.

A stunned silence filled the room and before anybody had time to speak, his secretary entered. With barely a glance, he said, 'Mrs Burrows, would you kindly see to it that the parents are escorted from the school premises please?'

If Nathan had been withdrawn and friendless before he'd decided to make the transition, his coming out didn't help. As

Natalie, she was now totally ostracised. I'd see her every day, sitting by herself in the canteen. Whenever she tried to sit with the other pupils, they'd just stand up and leave, passing remarks like, 'Let's move to another table, there's a queer smell around here.'

One afternoon, we'd finished English and were walking down the corridor to the science labs. As usual, Milly and I were dawdling when in front of us we saw Natalie stumble and fall, dropping all her books. I couldn't see what had happened, but I was certain someone had either pushed or tripped her. As if she wasn't there, everybody continued to walk, either around her or over her. Not one of her classmates offered to help her up. By the time we reached her, she was on her hands and knees scrambling to pick up her books and papers, which had been kicked along the corridor.

I said to Milly, 'I think we'd best help her.'

'Are you sure you want to help her? What will the rest of the class think? You know what they're saying about her!'

'Makes no difference what they think. You can't leave her struggling like this.' So, getting down on my hands and knees, I helped her pick up her books. Reluctantly, Milly joined in. I could see Natalie was upset and ready to start crying.

'Thank you very much,' she blubbered.

'No problem, we'll walk with you to the class if you like.' Then, looking at the time, I said, 'We'd best put our skates on, it looks like we're going to be late. You know what Mr Taylor's like for punctuality.'

When we arrived, everybody was sat at the benches with their lab coats and safety glasses on. Mr Taylor frowned and said, 'What time do you girls call this?'

I don't know if it was his use of the word "girls" that started them off, but once someone at the back started sniggering, the whole class followed. Mr Taylor angrily turned on the rest of the class and said, 'Did I say something funny?' There was no answer. Then he rounded on Sharon Dunkley and her two friends, Paige Logan and Stacey Walsh, who were still giggling, and said, 'Dunkley, did I just say something amusing?'

'No, sir,' she replied.

'If I didn't say anything funny, then someone must have.'

'It was Paige, sir, she was pulling funny faces and it made me laugh,'

'Okay, Logan, maybe you'd like to stand in the front of the class and pull one of your amusing faces. I'm sure they'd all enjoy it—that's if you can pull a funnier face than the one you already have.'

'I was trying to stop myself sneezing and that's why I kept pulling funny faces,' she lied.

'Either wipe those smirks off your faces or go to Mr Critchley's office and explain to him exactly what you find so amusing about my class.'

'Sorry, sir, it won't happen again,' said Paige.

'I hope not. Now sit down and concentrate on the worksheet you've got in front of you. Looking at me, Milly and Natalie, he said, 'As for you three, I want to see all of you at the end of the lesson. Now find a place so we can continue.'

When the lesson was over, we dutifully remained in our chairs until everyone had left. Mr Taylor kept his back to us as he busied himself cleaning the blackboard. He took an interminable time completing the task until he eventually turned round.

'Before I punish you, I'd like to know the reasons why the three of you were late for my lesson. It's not as if you didn't have enough time.'

'I'm sorry we were so late, it's all my fault,' I said, 'I got the timetable mixed up. I was looking at Thursday instead of Wednesday and thought we were doing drama. To be fair to Milly and Natalie, they kept on telling me they thought science was our next lesson, but I was so insistent that they followed me. It was only when we got to the theatre and didn't recognise any of the faces that the penny finally dropped. By this time, it was too late and we had to run as fast as we could to try and get here on time.'

'That's a wonderful story, Rosie. For a moment, I almost believed it myself, but I know what you're saying isn't true. Now tell me what really happened.'

'But it is the truth,' I protested.

'Don't believe her, she's not telling the truth,' protested Natalie. 'I fell over in the corridor, and Rosie and Milly were the only ones who were willing to stop and help me. They could easily have walked past me like all the others, but they didn't. Instead, they chose to stay with me to make sure I wasn't hurt. They picked up all my books and coursework and gave them back to me, then stayed with me till we finally arrived. And that's the real reason we were late.'

'From what I've heard, you didn't fall, you were tripped,' said Mr Taylor, 'and I've got a sneaking suspicion as to who was responsible. As for you, Rosie Brown, I'm surprised at you. I can't believe you had the temerity to stand in front of me and tell me barefaced lies. If there's one thing I can't stand, it's a liar. Fortunately for you, I believe you lied for all the right reasons; therefore, I'm prepared to overlook it. So the three of you can go, but next time, make sure you attend my classes on time.'

'Thank you, Mr Taylor,' we replied.

'It'll not happen again,' I added.

'I'll keep you to that. Now, on your way before I change my mind.'

We grabbed our things and hurriedly left the room. Once we were outside, I said, 'Good old Mr Taylor. He's not so bad after all. He may be strict, but he's fair. I don't know how he does it, but he always seems to know what's going on and who the troublemakers are.'

The school bell rang. It was time for home. We turned to say goodbye to Natalie, but she was nowhere to be seen. 'Where's she gone?' asked Milly.

'I don't know, she just vanished. Come on, Milly, no point in us hanging around, it's time we did our own disappearing act. Our mum's will be wondering where we are.'

The more I thought about it, the more I realised I'd never actually seen Natalie arrive or leave. I think she was scared of being bullied outside school so stayed behind to wait for her parents to pick her up.

CHAPTER SIX

I was beginning to wonder whether our good deed had been a wise move. Natalie began to follow us everywhere and would sit with us during lunch. I could see by her face Milly wasn't pleased about it. When Natalie was well out of earshot, she said, 'I don't think it's a good idea for us to be seen hanging around with Natalie, everyone's talking about us. Callum used to sit and have his lunch with us, but now that we've got Natalie in tow, he just ignores us. We've few enough friends as it is. The way things are going, we'll end up with no friends at all!'

'She may not be the kind of friend I'd have chosen, but like it or not, she's lonely and seems to have latched on to us and now I feel responsible for her. Anyway, she's a nice enough person. I haven't got the heart to just ignore her like all the others do. I mean ... what harm is she doing anyway?'

'Should we even be calling her Natalie?' Milly continued, 'shouldn't it be Nathan? After all, that's the name she was given at birth. As far as I'm concerned, she's just a boy wearing a girl's uniform.'

'That's not like you, Milly. I thought I knew you better than that! It's not up to us to start passing judgement, we don't know the torment she's been through or what's been going on inside her head. Genetically, she may be a boy, but that's not the point. It's what Natalie feels on the inside that really matters. If she feels she's a girl, wants to dress like a girl and be known by a girl's name, then what's so wrong with that? Let's face it, she's not harming anybody. After all, she's only human and as such, has the same feelings as the rest of us.'

'Since you put it that way, I suppose there isn't anything wrong with it, but I still can't help feeling a little bit uncomfortable whenever I'm in her company.'

'Shush... she's coming back.'

Natalie returned with a drink and sat with us. I could see Milly had a bee in her bonnet. Whatever I said or did, there was no way I was going to stop her. Sometimes I'd look at her and wonder whether Milly was suffering from some kind of hyperactivity syndrome. Whatever it was, one thing was certain, she was definitely a force of nature which, when unleashed, couldn't easily be stopped.

Instinctively, I knew Milly had set her mind on asking Natalie some awkward questions and I didn't know how I was going to divert her.

'Natalie...,' she began... 'when was it you decided you were Natalie and not Nathan?'

66

Natalie gave a huge sigh and her eyes clouded over. I could see this wasn't going to be easy for her. Taking a deep breath, she said, 'Ever since I can remember. I've always felt like I was a girl trapped in a boy's body.'

'I used to enjoy playing football with the rest of the kids in our street, but the only time I felt really happy was when I was wearing my sister's clothes and playing with her toys. My dad went beeswax when he found out, calling me a sissy. My mum was more relaxed about it, deciding it must be a phase I was going through and one I would eventually grow out of. But when I was old enough, I told them I was unhappy and wanted to change my sex. Dad put his foot down, overruled Mum and stopped me from dressing up. I became more and more depressed and started to self-harm. That's when they realised I needed help, so they had me referred to a gender identity clinic.'

'What's going to happen when you reach puberty?' I asked.

'That shouldn't happen,' said Natalie.

'Why's that?' asked Milly.

'Because I'm taking drugs to delay it.'

'Does that mean you're not taking any drugs to help you change into a girl?' continued Milly.

'No,' she replied.

Then she asked the most cringeworthy question of all!

'Do you still have little boy's bits?'

'Milly!' I said, as my face turned red, 'you shouldn't be asking embarrassing questions like that!'

'Why not?' asked Milly, 'Natalie's our friend, isn't she? I'm sure she doesn't mind me asking. You don't, do you, Natalie?'

'Milly's right, you're both my friends, so it's best you know everything about me. Just as long as you promise not to tell anyone else ... you won't, will you?'

She looked at us with pleading eyes as she waited for an answer. There was a long pause from Milly, who's not known for her tact, before I finally answered for both of us. I said, 'Yes, we promise. Don't we, Milly?' giving her a sharp kick on the shin.

'Yes,' she squealed.

'You're not just saying it, you really do promise you won't say a word to anyone?'

'Yes, we promise. DON'T WE, MILLY?' I said, raising my voice while giving her another sharp kick just to remind her.

'Yes,' she repeated, rubbing her shin.

Then Natalie whispered under her breath, 'Yes, I do still have boy's bits, but I'm not very happy about it. By law, I've got to wait until I'm sixteen before I can start making the change.'

Molly, in her own inimitable way, managed to sum up the whole conversation in one sentence. 'Then I suppose it's best you don't use our toilets and changing rooms... more's the pity!'

~~~

Natalie, for obvious reasons, never participated in PE and sport. She spent her time sitting in the library, reading and doing her homework. I didn't like the thought of her sat on her own and couldn't see any reason why she shouldn't come and play football with us, thinking it would boost her confidence. As both the boys and the girls wore the same football kit, there was no excuse for her to feel embarrassed. So, pulling her to one side, I said, 'Natalie... I've been thinking... why don't you come along and join us this Friday for a game of football? You'd have a great time and make new friends. It'd do you the world of good.'

'Thanks for asking, but somehow I don't think so.'

'Why don't you give it a try and see how it goes? If you find it's not to your liking, then you don't have to come again.'

'I'm not a sporty person, I'm a bit rusty on the rules, I've got two left feet, and I'd probably stick out like a sore thumb.'

'Most of the girls have never played football before, and as for the rules, Mr Preston tore up the rule book weeks ago in frustration when he first saw us playing. He said, "What's the point of a rule book when we keep making up our own?" So you'll be in good company. The fresh air will do you good, you'll have a great laugh and make new friends, it's a no brainer. Milly and I will be there so there's nothing for you to worry about and it'll put a bit of colour into your cheeks.' She promised to think it over and let me know.

Friday afternoon arrived but there was no sign of Natalie. When we ran out onto the playing field, the boys had already set up the nets and cones ready for us to practice our shooting and dribbling. Mr Preston gathered us together and gave us our instructions before nominating me to be coach, leaving me with a clipboard, a whistle and a stopwatch while he concentrated on the boys. That's when I heard a familiar voice from the touchline. 'Rosie... Milly... I'm here!' It was Natalie. She was wearing a United kit and football boots. 'Over here,' I shouted. Behind me I could hear the murmurs of disapproval.

Somebody mumbled, 'For God's sake, not her!'

Ignoring them, I beckoned her to join us. She came running over and stood next to me. None of the others said a word. Mr Preston, who was busy with the boys, hadn't seen Natalie's arrival. Clutching my clipboard, whistle and stopwatch, I took charge of the training. Setting the timer, I lined up the girls and sent them out one at a time, dribbling the ball through the cones.

'Very good, Ashleigh, twenty-nine seconds, much faster than last week. Okay, Jade, you're next.' I put all of the girls through their paces and without exception, they'd all improved from the previous week. 'Stacey,' I shouted, 'you were best of all, you completed the course in twenty-four seconds, well done.' Then I heard a voice next to me say, 'When's my turn?' It was Natalie.

'I thought I'd ease you into the training so you wouldn't get too downhearted if you didn't do as well as the rest of the girls. They've been training hard for weeks so you're going to find it difficult to keep up with them.'

'That's all right, I think I'll be able to do all that stuff without any problem.'

'If you're sure you'll be okay. I'll reset the timer and when I blow the whistle you do the same as the rest of the girls.'

She stood with a determined look on her face; it was a look I'd never seen before and one I didn't recognise. This wasn't at all like the shy retiring Natalie I'd come to know. She had a steely look in her eyes and was fully focused on the task at hand as she stood with her right foot perched on the ball, waiting for the whistle to blow. When I finally blew the whistle, I heard some of the girls catcalling and whistling. Natalie was possessed. She was like a greyhound out of the trap. The ball hardly left her feet as she weaved and turned through the cones as if they weren't there. Then she turned and returned without putting a foot wrong before finally stopping.

'How did I do?' said an exhausted Natalie.

I looked at the stopwatch, then gave it a shake and put it to my ear to check that it wasn't faulty.

'Well?' she gasped.

'Nineteen point five seconds exactly,' I said. The rest of the girls looked at each other in amazement.

Stacey, who'd previously been the quickest, said, 'Are you certain the time's correct?'

'Absolutely positive,' I replied, 'there's no mistake.'

Everyone stood and gaped, not quite believing what they'd just witnessed, while Natalie just blushed in embarrassment.

Okay, we'll set up the small nets, then we can do some shooting practice and we'll see who can score the most goals. Once again, it was Natalie who came out on top, scoring five goals from five attempts. Her rating among the other girls had slowly risen from something a dog dumps on the pavement to sneaking admiration.

That's when Mr Preston arrived. He'd not been witness to Natalie's prowess with a football, so he wasn't aware of her skills. When he saw her, he looked down his prominent nose, gave her a look of distain, then said, 'I see you've got a new girl in the team.' He emphasised the word girl, before continuing, 'You all know how we usually finish the training session, but for those who've not been here before...' Again, he looked at Natalie. '...We always finish with a girls versus boys football game. The rules are the same as before. You should all know what they are by now—ten minutes each half.'

'I hope it's not going to be like last week when the ref kept bending the rules in favour of the girls,' mumbled someone at the back.

'Who said that?' shouted Mr Preston.

Nobody spoke.

'I'll give the person who said that one last chance to own up!'

Still nobody spoke.

'This is your last chance to own up or else there'll be no more football today!'

A voice from the back called out, 'Sorry, sir, it was me, it just slipped out.' It was Jordan Moss.

'That's a yellow card for you, Moss,' he said, waving it in the air.

'That's not fair, sir, why did I get a yellow?'

'For dissent,' he replied, 'you're lucky it wasn't red. Okay, when you're all ready. It's the girls' turn to kick off.'

I wasn't sure whether Natalie's success on the training ground had been a fluke or not so, not wanting her to get hurt, I decided to put her on the wing.

Inevitably, the boys eventually gained possession, passing it between each other, never allowing us into the game. Halfway into the second half, they decided it was time to take their foot off the brake. They were still smarting from last week's defeat which, to be fair, was due in no small part to some dubious refereeing decisions by Mr Preston.

From the corner of my eye, I saw Callum give the goalie a quick nod and point to the far corner. As soon as he received the ball, the goalie kicked it long and high to where Callum had indicated. As usual, our defenders were clueless. They just stood and watched as Callum raced onto the ball. All he had to do was collect it and he'd score.

In desperation, I screamed, 'Somebody stop him' in the vain hope he'd slip and fall. They say if you believe in miracles then sometimes they happen.

To my amazement, Natalie appeared as if from nowhere. Somehow, she'd heard my plea and managed to sprint back in time to collect the ball before Callum could reach it. Skipping past him as if he wasn't there, she went hurtling down the wing.

Now the boot was on the other foot. Angry and frustrated, unable to comprehend what had just occurred, Callum shouted, 'Stop her!' But by now she was in full flight, ball firmly glued to her feet. One of the boys shouted furiously, 'It's that bleeding queer, chop his legs from under him!' Suddenly, Natalie was public enemy number one with a lynch mob in hot pursuit.

The first to reach her threw himself feet first at her spindly legs. Natalie, poised and balanced, casually stroked the ball along the touchline before leaping gazelle-like to avoid what would have been a leg breaking tackle.

Gathering the ball, she continued her run, only to be confronted by two more irate opponents. Nutmegging the first and dancing past the second, she continued her relentless run only to find two burly defenders ahead of her. Unnoticed, I'd managed to make a run through the centre of the field and was homing in on the goal, so I shouted, 'To me, Natalie.'

Cool as a cucumber, she floated the ball over their heads and into the goal area where yours truly, having just arrived, gathered the ball and slotted it past their bemused goalkeeper. 1-0 for the girls. To our relief, Mr Preston blew the whistle, shouting, 'Game over, the girls have won!'

'That's unfair, sir,' moaned a despondent Callum, 'there's still some time left on the clock.'

'I'm the one who says how long the game lasts and I say it's over. And as for you lot,' he said, gesticulating towards rest of the boys, 'I'm totally disgusted with the way you acted today. I want to see you all outside the head's office first thing Monday morning!'

'That's not fair, sir, what have we done wrong?'

'I think you know exactly what you've done wrong, and frankly I'm ashamed and disgusted with the lot of you! You've got the whole of the weekend to think about how you conducted yourselves today, and I hope when I see you again you've had enough time to reflect on your actions and can provide me with a good excuse as to why I shouldn't punish you.'

We hadn't heard any of this, we were too busy celebrating our win on the other side of the pitch.

'Natalie,' I said, 'where did you learn to play football like that?'

'I've always enjoyed having a kick around with the rest of the kids,' she said nonchalantly.

'You were brilliant. Once you got into your stride, there was no way they were ever going to touch you. You could see by their faces they were gutted. They thought they could spend their time messing around then score a couple of goals at the end of the game to beat us, but they never reckoned on us having a secret weapon. Natalie, you were out of this world! I hope you're going to continue training with us, We may be a bit rough around the edges but the way the team's taking shape, I really believe we'll soon be as good as, if not better than, the boys.'

We were all on a high as we walked back to the changing rooms chanting, 'We beat the boys, we beat the boys, ee aye adio, we beat the boys' while Natalie quietly disappeared into the building. This time nobody bothered to comment on where she'd gone or what she was doing. It didn't seem to matter anymore. What had previously been the subject of ridicule had, during the course of one momentous afternoon, changed into a grudging respect tinged with admiration for her bravery.

Before she left, Mr Preston took Natalie to one side and said to her, 'You're a very good player for your age, how would you like to start playing in the boys' team?'

'I'm not even certain I want to play for the girls. let alone the boys, replied Natalie, 'but if I do decide, it'll probably be with the girls.'

'You're too good for the girls' team, it seems such a shame to waste all that natural talent. I'll tell you what, I'll give you till

76

next Friday to think about it, then you can give me your final decision.'

~~~

Monday morning and the boys' football team was waiting outside Mr Critchley's door. Mr Preston had already given his report on the events of Friday afternoon. A buzzer sounded and Mrs Burrows picked up the phone. Listening to the voice on the other end, she answered, 'I'll send them in.'

'If you'll follow me, Mr Critchley will see you now.'

She crossed to his office, opened the door, then stood to one side as the boys sheepishly trooped in.

'That will be all, Mrs Burrows. I'll send for you when I've finished.'

Turning, she closed the door behind her. They waited in uncomfortable silence for Mr Critchley to finish reading. Behind him, wearing his tracksuit and whistle, arms crossed and stoney faced, stood Mr Preston. It didn't take a genius to know why they were there.

Mr Critchley placed the papers on his desk and, looking over his glasses, said, 'I thought I made myself perfectly clear when I said I wasn't prepared to tolerate any form of intolerance or bullying, especially where Natalie Morris is concerned. Sadly, it seems to have fallen on deaf ears. The reason you're here is, I've received a report regarding a serious incident which occurred during the boys versus girl's football match on Friday afternoon where Natalie Morris, who was playing for the girls' team, was subjected to an unacceptable level of violence and abuse. The perpetrators were described as acting like a pack of baying hounds whose sole intention was to seriously injure Natalie, shouting, and I quote, "It's that bleeding queer, chop his legs from under him."'

'Somehow, Natalie managed to rise above it, evading your malicious tackles and, in the words of Mr Preston, "Ran rings round you." Luckily, no one was injured or you'd now be facing criminal charges. As of yet, I've not had a chance to speak to Natalie; I don't even know if she was aware of your evil intentions. Should she decide to press charges, I can assure you she'll have our full support.'

'I can't stress strongly enough the seriousness of this matter and intend to interview everybody who was witness to this outrageous spectacle to ascertain whether disciplinary action should be taken. As you were all to some extent involved, until further notice I've decided to disband the boys' football team!' Mr Critchley paused and an audible groan filled the room. Then he continued, 'Pending a full report, this meeting is now adjourned. You may now return to your classes!'

Back in class, Mr Bolton was busy taking the register and it was becoming increasingly apparent some of the boys were missing. It was no coincidence they were the same boys who'd been playing football on Friday. Once again, Natalie was the topic of conversation, but this time for the right reasons. Natalie's standing in school was at an all-time high, especially among the girls.

Jade, who'd previously shunned her, said, 'Well done, Natalie, you certainly showed them how to play football.'

'Congratulations, Natalie,' said another, 'that'll put those big heads in their place.'

There was a knock on the door and in walked the missing boys. Mr Bolton had already been briefed by Mr Critchley and was aware of the situation, 'Please remain standing until registration is complete,' he instructed.

They looked pale and worried. Once registration was over, Mr Bolton turned to the boys and said, 'Although I've not been given the full details, from the information I've so far received, I believe an apology is in order!'

Following an awkward silence, Callum stepped forward, looked Natalie straight in the eye and said, 'Me and the rest of the lads want to apologise for our behaviour. What we did was bang out of order. We promise we'll never act in that way ever again and hope you'll accept our apology.'

Natalie looked deeply embarrassed. All she could do was mumble something inaudible, which everyone took to be, 'Thank you.'

'Oh, and by the way, you played a brilliant game of footie on Friday!' concluded Callum.

'Okay, boys, back to your desks,' said Mr Bolton.

All eyes were now on Natalie, whose normally pallid complexion had turned a deep shade of crimson. As they walked past her, each of the boys gave her a tap on the shoulder and said, 'Sorry, Natalie!'

CHAPTER SEVEN

Weeks turned into months. Sightings of Dad became less and less. During this time, the police paid regular visits to our house, usually on the pretext they were keeping us updated on the results of their search. But I wasn't convinced. I felt certain they suspected Mum was involved in the fraud and knew where Dad was hiding. Some evenings I'd look out of my window and see the same old scruffy black car parked down the road. I'd occasionally see faces illuminated by the light of their mobile phones. They didn't look much like policemen to me, but then again, if they were working undercover, you wouldn't expect them to. The fact remained—they were watching us. But something in my head kept saying, What if they aren't policemen? This then begged the question, If they're not police, then who are they?

On Saturday afternoon, Inspector Maitland made one of his 'surprise' visits. Why he always chose Saturdays, I'll never know. He appeared to have taken a bit of a shine to Mum. I suspected this could be a ploy to get her to drop her guard and reveal Dad's whereabouts.

She was obviously flattered by his attention and he knew it. Over the past few weeks, she'd started looking forward to his visits. She'd spend the preceding hour bathing and applying just enough makeup to make herself presentable yet appealing. After all, she didn't want him to think she had the hots for him. But no, nothing could be further from the truth!

As expected, the knock came.

'I wonder who that could be?' said Mum, as if she didn't know.

'Shall I answer it, Mum?' I shouted, knowing she wouldn't let me.

'No, sweetheart, you've got homework to do... I'll answer it.'

I'd pretend to go to my room then stand at the top of the stairs eavesdropping.

I watched as Mum opened the door. 'Why if it isn't Inspector Maitland,' said Mum, 'what a pleasant surprise!'

'I just happened to be in the area,' he said, 'and I thought I'd pop round to return your husband's laptop. CID has finished with it now.'

'Did they find anything?' queried Mum.

'Our computer bods used every trick in the book to crack the password, but with little success. They even asked Apple for help, but they refused.'

'Couldn't you have issued a court order on them?' asked Mum.

'They're not based in the UK, so we don't have jurisdiction over them.' Then, in a stern voice, he asked, 'Are you absolutely certain he didn't give you his password?'

'I've told you before, due to the confidential information it contained, he never allowed anybody to use his laptop.'

The inspector's face hardened further and as if reciting from a script, he said, 'I'm obliged to warn you, it is a criminal offence to withhold any information which may be of assistance to the police in the furtherance of their enquiries. Failure to do so could result in a prison sentence.'

'I can only reiterate,' said Mum, angrily, 'that he NEVER disclosed his password to anyone!'

Then the inspector said, cheerily, 'Can't stay too long, duty calls and all that.'

'You're welcome to come in and take the weight off your feet,' said Mum as if the altercation had never happened.

Looking at his watch, he said, 'I think I can spare a few minutes.'

'I'll put the kettle on—strong with two sugars, and plenty of milk as I recall.'

'You've got a marvellous memory, Mrs Brown. Exactly how I like it.'

'Rosie,' Mum called, 'I'm making a cup of tea for the inspector, do you want one,'

'Yes,' I shouted, 'I'll be right down!'

Mum returned with a plate of digestives and three steaming mugs of tea, then set them down on the coffee table.

I deliberately faced the telly, pretending to be watching old reruns of Dancing on Ice, while in reality I was listening intently to their conversation.

Inspector Maitland sat in the chair Mum always reserved for visitors. He looked uncomfortable in his uniform.

'Would you like a biscuit with your tea, inspector,' asked Mum.

'That would be lovely,' he replied.

With my tongue sticking out and index fingers firmly lodged in the cheeks of my mouth, I pulled one of my 'it's enough to make you want to vomit' faces.

'Are you okay, Rosie?' asked Inspector Maitland, who'd obviously seen me out of the corner of his eye. 'You've turned a funny colour.'

Realising he'd clocked me making fun of him, I started to blush profusely. I ought to have known that as a serving police officer, he'd be well versed in the art of reading facial expressions.

'It's probably me wincing in horror at Bez trying to skate. You should have seen him, it was hilarious,' I hastily improvised, 'he tried a jump, went flying through the air, lost his balance and landed flat on his arse.'

'Rosie, how dare you use language like that in front of Inspector Maitland. Go to your room at once!'

I lingered at the top of the stairs just long enough to hear the inspector saying, 'Don't be too hard on Rosie,' before I defiantly shouted, 'I only said arse,' then slammed the door behind me.

Meanwhile, downstairs, Mum tried to apologise, but the inspector was adamant. 'No need to apologise, Rosie's a good girl. I've seen children much older than her go completely off the rails over far less than she's been through.'

Changing the subject, Mum said, 'Drink your tea, inspector, it's getting cold.'

'Please, don't call me inspector... call me Nigel.'

'Okay... Nigel, but you must start calling me Mavis.'

'Okay... Mavis.'

Dangling the bait, she continued, 'I suppose you'll be taking your wife out for a meal tonight?'

Heaving a huge sigh, he replied, 'I'm afraid there isn't a Mrs Maitland... there never has been. Too wrapped up in my work, I suppose. An empty house and a microwave are all I have to look forward to.'

'You poor thing. It can't be very healthy eating those horrible ready meals. I'm making dinner for me and Rosie tonight, why don't you join us? It's just as easy cooking for three as it is for two.'

'That's very kind of you, Mavis,' he replied, 'but I'm afraid I'll have to refuse. I need to pop back to the station to complete my report. The guv wants it on his desk first thing Monday morning. As well as returning the laptop,' he continued. 'I also wanted to update you on our investigations. We did receive further sightings of your husband, but they didn't lead to anything.'

He sat and talked a little while longer, then made his excuses and left.

After he'd gone, Mum shouted, 'You can come down now, dinner will be ready soon.'

'He's certainly got the hots for you, Mum,' I said, casually.

'Don't be silly,' she flushed, 'he's only trying to keep us in the loop.' Then, quickly changing the subject, she said, 'If you help me clear the table, I'll wash the dishes.'

'Leave them on the drainer when you're finished and I'll dry them,' I replied.

Once we'd tidied up, I went upstairs, put on my pyjamas and dressing gown, then joined Mum on the sofa to watch telly.

'Sorry for being so horrid to the inspector,' I said, 'I don't know what came over me. When he's not in uniform, he's probably a nice man.'

'That's okay, I'm sure he understands.'

At ten o'clock, Mum said, 'Okay, Rosie, get yourself washed and into bed and I'll bring you up some supper.'

When Mum came in, I was sat in waiting. 'I've made you crackers, cheese and cocoa,' she said. 'Be careful, though, it's still hot. I'll be back later when you've finished.'

I don't know what it is about cocoa, but as soon as I've drunk it, I start feeling drowsy.

I was almost asleep when Mum returned. Silently, she tucked me in and kissed my forehead. She was about to close the door when I called to her, 'Can you leave the door open please, Mum?'

Ever since we'd lived here, I'd never felt comfortable sleeping in this room. If I believed in ghosts, I'd swear it was haunted. One thing was irrefutable, it was the coldest room in the house. I didn't want to burden Mum with my fears—she had enough on her plate as it was—but still, for some reason, this room gave me the creeps. Sometimes at night, I'd imagine shadowy figures watching me from the darkest recesses of my room. I was always relieved to hear the comforting sound of Mum's footsteps on the stairs when she finally came to bed.

It had been a long day and to put it crudely, I was cream crackered. All talk of Dad must have preyed on my mind. I buried my head beneath the covers and fell into a deep sleep, only to be rudely awakened by the sound of somebody calling my name. Sitting bolt upright, I peered into the shadows. 'Dad... is that you?' I softly called.

An eerie silence descended. Outside, the streetlights flickered then died, plunging the room into darkness. I strained my ears but there wasn't a sound. I looked at the time; it was almost twelve. I'd hoped to hear the reassuring ticking of the clock, but the hands had frozen. Only the second hand displayed signs of life, flicking backwards and forwards as if suspended in time. From beyond the confines of the room, a distant voice called out, 'Please help me, I'm hungry and cold.' It was Dad's voice, of that I was sure, and it was coming from deep within the darkest corner of my room.

I cried out, 'Don't worry, Dad, I'm coming.' Despite my foreboding, I knew, if I were to find him, I'd have to face whatever terrors lay within that corner. Heart pounding, I climbed out of bed and gingerly made my way to the place I feared the most—the place inhabited by the shadowy figures. As I reached the portal, my heart began to pound. Should I or shouldn't I? With Dad out there somewhere and needing my help, what other option did I have?

Once I crossed the threshold, there'd be no turning back. Deep within the void, the swirling blackness was all pervading, enfolding me with its inky tentacles. Blindly, I held out my arms and felt my way ahead.

I should have reached the corner by now, I thought.

Undaunted, I continued to wade through the dense blackness. Suddenly, I had the overwhelming urge to turn and run, but having long since lost my sense of direction, where could I run to? Ahead, Dad's voice kept beckoning me. 'Hurry up, Rosie, I can't hold on much longer!'

No matter what perils lay ahead, if I were to find him, I had to continue my journey.

The transition from night to day was instantaneous. As my eyes adjusted to the brightness, I found myself standing in a quiet country lane. From out of nowhere, a faceless cyclist approached. He stopped and pointed to a gap in the drystone wall, where a rusty signpost proclaimed, 'Old Man of Coniston, 5 Miles'. Clambering over the stile, I followed the path until I reached a derelict building. I decided to stop and catch my breath and was about to continue when a distant voice came echoing down the mountainside, 'I'm up here, Rosie.' It was Dad!

The lower sections of the railway had long since been buried under a mountain of rock and debris. To reach what remained, my only option was to climb a steep slope.

Buoyed by the prospect of finding Dad, I scrambled to the top then followed its tortuous route. Like a coiled snake, the railway clung to the contours as it slowly clawed its way uphill. My uneventful journey was brought to an abrupt halt when I reached a collapsed section of track. All that remained was a narrow ledge and one forlorn sleeper perilously clinging to a piece of twisted rail.

Undeterred, I pressed myself against the cliff face and stepped out onto the ledge. Buffeted by a strong wind, I closed my eyes, gritted my teeth and groped my way to the other side. Once on firm ground, I continued my trek until I arrived at a disused mine. The entrance was shuttered and boarded with a sign warning, 'Danger No Entry'. Peering through the wooden slats, I bellowed, 'Are you in there, Dad?'

There came a loud rumble, followed by a blast of hot foul air, knocking me off my feet. Thinking I'd inadvertently caused a mine collapse, I waited until the dust had settled, then listened. At first I heard nothing, then a faint voice croaked, 'Is that you, Rosie? I've been waiting for you.' Excitedly, I called out, 'Yes, it's me.'

If Dad were down there, he'd need my help, so without further hesitation, I pulled away the rotting timbers and clambered through the gap. I then descended into the blackness. The deeper I went, the more I began to doubt myself. I can't see Dad being daft enough to come down here, I thought.

Seeing the logic of my argument, and the fact that I was wet, cold and still hadn't found Dad, I decided it was time to call it a day. That's when I heard a pitiful cry… 'Help me, Rosie.'

Casting logic to the wind, I was determined to continue.

As I became accustomed to the light, I was aware of something propped up against the wall. Taking a torch from my bag, I switched it on, but the stupid thing just flickered and died. I gave it a couple of clouts and it resentfully responded with a faint beam of light. 'Bloody batteries!' I grumbled.

Moving closer, I saw what appeared to be a shop mannequin. 'Dad, is that you?' I optimistically whispered.

I'd been too preoccupied to notice the rotten smell, but the nearer I got, the stronger it became. I shone the rapidly fading beam into the mannequin's face then recoiled in horror. It was Dad, but not as I remembered him. His eyes were bulging and his mouth twisted in a deathly grimace. His eyes started to move and for one crazy moment I thought he might still be alive. I watched in horror as his eyes slowly increased in size, Then, to my disgust, propelled by a stream of maggot-filled gunge, they popped out of their sockets and landed in a writhing mass at my feet. Emitting an ear-piercing scream, I dropped the torch. As I turned to run, I lost my footing, landing flat on my back in the middle of a stream of slurry. Unable to get to my feet, I felt myself slowly, irreversibly, sliding into the deepest, darkest recesses of the tunnel.

I woke in a pool of sweat to the sound of Mum running across the landing. 'Are you all right, Rosie? I thought I heard a scream.' Switching on the light, she said, 'Just look at you, you're soaking wet, take off those pyjamas while I get you some clean ones from the airing cupboard.'

'I've just seen Dad,' I said, panting in fear, 'it was horrible, he was dead and his body was rotting away.'

'You've been having a nightmare,' she said, reassuringly. 'It's all my fault, I shouldn't have given you cheese before you went to bed. Now put these clean pyjamas on and try to get some rest. I'll leave the landing light on just in case, but if you still can't sleep you can come and sleep with me.'

CHAPTER EIGHT

I'd always suspected the people watching our house were police officers. All I needed was the opportunity to prove it.

'Me plates are killing me,' groaned Mum, 'I've been on me feet all day. How they expect you to arrive at a client's house at eight, get her up, washed, dressed, and fed, then be at the next house by eight thirty is beyond me.'

Seeing I was stifling a yawn, she said, 'Sorry, love, I must be boring you. Tell you what, why don't I leave you in peace and go upstairs for a nice long soak?'

'You're not boring me, Mum,' I protested, 'I'm just a bit tired, that's all.'

I waited until I heard her running the bath then I quietly opened the front door and peered out into the street. Sure enough, there they were—Snitch & Snatch, slumped in their seats, each clutching industrial strength vaping machines as they attempted to break the record for the largest ever vaping cloud.

I've got to hand it to them, they're nothing if not persistent.

I knew, once Mum was in the bath, it'd be a long time before she finally resurfaced. So I decided, if I were going to turn the tables on them, it was now or never.

Wearing hiking boots, old jeans and an ill-fitting camouflage jacket, I sneaked out of the backdoor and across the yard. Knowing the slightest noise could instigate a cacophony of barking, I silently slipped open the bolt, lifted the latch, opened the gate, and stepped out onto the cobble stone alley.

I threaded my way through numerous hazards and obstacles until I finally reached the lights of Gerard Street. That's when I smelt it. Looking down, I found a particularly disgusting slab of dog dirt had attached itself to the sole of my boot. Using the edge of the kerb as a makeshift scraper, I managed to remove as much of the foul smelling stuff as I could, then hurried to the corner to survey the scene. And to my relief, I found the car hadn't moved.

Although my vantage point provided a clear view of the street, I still couldn't identify the car's occupants. Having spied an open curtain, the passenger, after swapping his vape for binoculars, had trained them on Cheryl at number three's bedroom window. Seemingly oblivious to his pervy partner's voyeurism, the driver sat idly scrolling through his iPhone. To get a clearer view of the occupants, I pulled the hood of my jacket tightly over my head and ambled across the street, then casually sauntered towards them.

When I was close enough, I stopped, knelt and pretended to fasten my bootlaces. From this position, I was able to gain a clearer view of the occupants.

The passenger was much younger than the driver. He had black, greasy hair, a brown, weatherbeaten face and he wore a black polo-necked sweater beneath a scruffy bronze effect bomber jacket. There was something vaguely familiar about him —something that scared me. Then I remembered where I'd seen him. He'd been part of a group of itinerants suspected of plying underage girls with drugs and drink while they were working for a travelling funfair. The story was reported in the local newspaper along with a photo of him and his accomplices standing behind a group of screaming girls on the Waltzer. There were also unsubstantiated rumours of vulnerable children mysteriously disappearing after the funfair had been to town.

Mum made me read and reread the article, then warned me of the dangers of wandering round fairgrounds on my own, especially at night. It all happened a few years ago but even now it haunts my dreams. Ever since then I've had a morbid fear of funfairs.

In stark contrast, the driver was well groomed, in his late fifties, with short, wavy hair and a teasy weasy moustache, hinting at a military background. He looked every bit the dapper in his barathea blazer, white shirt, cravat, and trilby. He reminded me of the man who'd sold Mum the old banger; the man she always referred to as 'that effin spiv'. Whatever their occupations, one thing was certain, unless they were spectacularly good at undercover work, they had nothing to do with the police. The spiv stopped what he was doing and slowly began to eye me up. My pathetic attempt at looking inconspicuous had only succeeded in arousing his suspicion. Giving 'fairground' a nudge, he whispered in his ear, then pointed at me. Now they were both regarding me. Lowering my head, I got to my feet, pulled the hood further over my face, then nonchalantly ambled past the car, hoping I'd remain unrecognised. That's when the spiv said, 'Fergie—isn't that the Brown girl?'

'Fairground' fixed me with a cold hard stare and waited until I was close, then exclaimed, 'You're right, Ted. It is her. She must be on to us—let's get her!'

I'd heard enough to know that if I didn't move quickly, they'd grab me and bundle me into the car. Turning on my heels, I started legging it up the street. You didn't have to be a fitness expert to see Ted was no athlete, but Fergie was a different matter. Lean, mean and built like a robber's dog, he was soon out of the blocks and giving chase. I felt confident that once I'd established a healthy lead, I'd be difficult to catch. When I reached the end of terrace, I paused briefly to glance round, and to my dismay, I found Fergie breathing down my neck. Cursing my choice of footwear, I rounded the corner, only to clatter into a random wheelie bin, knocking me off my stride.

With the alley beckoning and Fergie only milliseconds away, my only hope of escape was to find a way of stopping him in his tracks. In desperation, I grabbed the wheelie bin and flung it across the pavement. As soon as he turned the corner, Fergie's eyes lit up. 'Gotcha,' he growled. Unfortunately, he'd failed to notice there was an obstacle blocking his path. Unable to stop, he ran straight into the bin, went flying through the air, then landed with a resounding thud on the unforgiving flagstones.

Obviously in no fit state to continue, I walked over to him and taunted, 'Serves you right.' Then I turned and ran, closely followed by a string of obscenities.

My best chance of avoiding capture was finding somewhere to hide. As I ran, I pushed at every gate along the alley. That's when I stood on something big, soft, black, and furry. It was Mrs Finnegan's moggy, Maxwell. It was hard to say which of us was more surprised, him or me. It certainly wasn't the greeting he'd been expecting. Screeching loudly, he disappeared over the nearest wall while I, trying to maintain my balance, continued running.

To my surprise, the very next gate I tried flew open and I went tumbling into the backyard. Quickly regaining my composure, I silently closed the gate and awaited their arrival.

A car drew up and an indistinct voice called out.

'What's happened to you, Fergie?'

'What the hell does it look like?'

'Don't tell me she got away.'

'It wouldn't have happened if you'd got here sooner.'

'It still doesn't explain why you're lying on the floor with your knees poking out of your trackies.'

'That Brown girl,' growled Fergie, 'she's smarter than I thought.'

'How come a spotty faced kid like her managed to outwit a meathead like you?'

'I underestimated her. That's all.'

'It doesn't take much to outsmart you, does it Fergie?'

'If you're so clever, then how come it took you so long to get here?'

'I thought I'd hang about for a while, just in case she decided to double back.'

'What you actually mean is, you were too lazy to get off your jacksie!'

'Motors are my business and what pays your wages, Fergie?' growled Ted, 'and don't you forget it. Anyway, I'm built for comfort not speed!'

'I can see that!'

Fergie tried to stand... then collapsed. 'I think I must have torn a muscle or something, can you give me a hand?'

Reluctantly, Ted clambered out of the car and walked to where Fergie was sitting. 'Grab hold and I'll help you to the car.'

Before Fergie had time to flop down into the front seat, Ted pointed into the back of the car and said, 'See that tartan rug?'

'Yes,' groaned Fergie.

'Do me a favour and throw it over the passenger seat.'

'What for?'

'I don't want blood all over my upholstery.'

'You're all heart, aren't you?'

'It has been commented upon,' smirked Ted.

Once he was finally able to sit down, Fergie asked Ted, 'The Brown girl should be home by now; do you think she'll call the cops?'

'She's bound to,' replied Ted.

'Then we best not waste any more time.'

Adding a note of caution, Ted said, 'After tonight, I think we ought to lie low until the dust settles.'

Fergie winced as he fastened his seatbelt, then groaned, 'Step on it, Ted, I need to get back to my place and sort myself out.'

Ted glanced at him, then said, 'That's a nasty looking lump you've got on your head, Fergie. Don't you think you'd be better off going to A&E just in case you've got concussion?'

'Nah, it's only a bump. I've had far worse than this outside Spoons on a Saturday night.'

'You know what they say, Fergie?'

'What's that, Ted?'

'Where there's no sense, there's no feeling!'

99

~~~

I only caught snatches of their conversation, but what little I heard was enough to tell me they were dangerous criminals. Still reeling from my encounter with Fergie, I decided to rest up for a while and try to make sense of the situation.

Who the heck were they?

Why had they been watching our house?

What were they looking for?

And crucially... should I tell Mum about them?

As I pondered these questions, a light came on in the kitchen, closely followed by a key turning in a lock. Making a hurried retreat, I slipped out of the gate and quietly closed it behind me... then waited. From within the yard, a gravelly voice croaked, 'Maxwell, is that you?' It was Mrs Finnegan. She'd obviously heard the commotion and came out to investigate. Unable to resist, and utilising my best cat impersonation, I answered... 'Meow?'

With the coast clear, I made my way to our gate and slipped into the yard, firmly bolting the gate behind me. I'd hardly closed the back door before Mum came bursting into the kitchen. When she saw me in my jacket and boots, she yelled, 'Where the hell have you been?'

'Just out the back,' I replied, meekly.

'What's so urgent you have to go out at this time of night?'

'I lost some exercise books on the way home from school,' I continued, 'and thought I'd check the back alley to see if they'd fallen out of my bag.'

'And had they?' she grilled.

'Yes, they're a bit dirty, but they'll soon clean up.'

'And while we're on the subject of the back alley,' she continued, 'what's that awful pong?'

'What pong?' I said, innocently.

'THAT pong,' she reiterated. 'If you ask me, it smells like dog muck. Show me the soles of your boots, young lady!' Grabbing one ankle, then the other, she said, 'Just as I thought, you've been standing in dog dirt!'

That's when she noticed the doormat and a trail of footprints across the floor. 'The whole kitchen's caked in it! I hope you've not trodden it through the rest of the house.'

'I've not been anywhere else, only in here,' I assured her.

'What have I told you about walking down that alley?' she fumed, 'especially at night. It looks like you've managed to find every turd in the alley.'

With hands on hips, she surveyed the mess, then said, 'If you think I'm going to clean this lot up, you've got another thing coming. I've only just got out of the bath, so you're going to have to do it yourself. When you're finished, take off your boots and leave them outside the back door. I'll sort them out in the morning. In the meantime, get a mop and a bucket of hot water with plenty of disinfectant in it and make a start on the floor. When you're finished, I don't want to see or smell a single hint of dog muck!'

'Aww, Mum... that's not fair,' I pleaded, 'it's going to take me ages. I've still got my homework to do and worst of all, I'll end up stinking of disinfectant for the rest of the night.'

'You should've thought of that before deciding to go wandering down back alleys in the dark. Anyhow, it's better than smelling of dog dirt, and a heck of a lot cleaner. While you're busy doing that, I'll run another bath and put a nice smelly bath bomb in it.'

After I'd had my bath, I put on my PJs and sneaked into the box room. Standing with my back against the wall, I peeped both up and down the street, but there was no sign of them.

How could I tell Mum what had happened? How I'd sneaked out to spy on them. How they'd chased me down the alley. And how I'd only managed to make it back by the skin of my teeth. She probably wouldn't have believed me anyway and in the unlikely event she did, she'd only have got scared and wouldn't be able to sleep for worrying. That night I found sleep elusive. Having recently overcome my fear of that stupid corner, I now had something new to worry about. I kept wondering just exactly who Ted and Fergie were and why they were watching our house. If Fergie and the man in the newspaper were one and the same, then why was a dangerous criminal like him watching our house? It's not as if we're loaded. In fact, Mum's always saying, 'We've not got two ha'pennies to rub together', so if it was money they were after, they were wasting their time. No matter how hard I tried, I couldn't shake off the uneasy feeling it had something to do with Dad's shady financial dealings.

CHAPTER NINE

I knew the day would eventually arrive. It's funny, but no matter how much you prepare for the inevitable, it still comes as a shock.

We were in the middle of a history lesson when Mrs Burrows knocked and entered. She walked up to Mrs Dean and whispered in her ear. Mrs Dean looked over her glasses and beckoned me to the front, then whispered, 'Rosie, can you stop what you're doing and accompany Mrs Burrows to the principal's office please?'

What had I done wrong? I know I can be a bit stubborn and headstrong whenever there's a matter of principle at stake, but just recently I'd had very little time to get involved in classroom politics. I'd been spending most of my time studying for my exams, so it came as a shock to be abruptly uprooted from the class and summoned to the principal's office.

Maintaining a brisk pace, I soon found myself trailing in her wake. When I finally caught up with her, I said, 'Excuse me, Mrs Burrows, do you know what this is all about?'

'I'm not at liberty to disclose anything, you'll have to wait until you see the principal.'

When we arrived at the outer office, Mrs Burrows pointed to a chair and I dutifully sat down. Positioning herself behind the desk, she picked up the phone and said, 'Mr Critchley, Rosemary Brown's in the office, shall I send her in?' She listened intently to the muffled voice on the other end then, putting the phone down, she said, 'Mr Critchley's not quite ready yet, he'll only be a few minutes.'

It seemed like an eternity before the phone rang. 'Yes, Mr Critchley... certainly Mr Critchley... I'll send her in now Mr Critchley.'

'If you're ready, Rosemary, Mr Critchley will see you now.'

When I entered the office, Mr Critchley was sat behind his desk. He had a grim look on his face. I was surprised to see he was accompanied by an official looking man with a dour face. 'I think you'd better sit down, Rosie,' said Mr Critchley, 'Sergeant Baines would like to have a word with you.' Whatever I'd done, surely it wasn't serious enough for the police to become involved.

Sergeant Baines shuffled uncomfortably in his chair as he rummaged through his attaché case, before removing a file. He paused, thumbed through some papers then, looking me in the eyes, he said, 'Rosie... I've got something to tell you.' Then, taking a deep breath, he said, 'We believe we may have found your father.' Not knowing what to say next, I blurted out excitedly, 'Where is he... is he okay... when can I see him?'

'I'm afraid it's not good news. It seems a group of ramblers out on a walk got caught in a hail storm and were forced to take shelter in a disused mine. While they were waiting, one of them decided to venture further inside and came upon the body of a man. Subsequent enquiries have led us to conclude the body may be that of your father. Your mother's been informed and is currently at the mortuary identifying the body.'

'Can I go with her to see him?' I asked.

'It's possible the body may not be that of your father. When they found the body, it was already in an advanced state of decomposition. It's not a very pleasant sight for an adult to witness let alone a young girl like yourself.'

Mr Critchley brought the conversation to a conclusion, saying, 'Rosie? Sergeant Baines has kindly volunteered to take you home so if you want, you may go to your locker and gather your things together. We'll be waiting for you in my office.'

As the car pulled up outside our house, I noticed the curtains were drawn. Inspector Baines knocked on the door and Mum answered. She had a tissue in her hand. Her eyes were red and puffy and her makeup was smudged. 'Is it true, Mum... have they found Dad?'

'Yes, it's true. I've just come back from the mortuary and there's no doubt about it.'

I don't know why, but I was unable to cry. All I felt was a numbness and an intense feeling of loss. Deep down inside, I'd been preparing myself for this day, having already come to terms with the fact Dad was never coming back. I'd felt certain if Dad were still alive, he'd have found a way of making contact before now.

~~~

The coroner was informed and a post mortem ordered. When it was completed, Dad's body was released for burial. On the day of the funeral, the coffin was brought from the chapel of rest to our house. Mum and I were waiting, ready to take our places in the back of a black limousine and follow the hearse to the crematorium, where a brief, non-denominational ceremony was to be held in the chapel. Dad had been brought up a Roman Catholic, but somewhere along the way, he'd lost his faith.

On numerous occasions, he'd expressed the desire not to have a church service. His actual words were, 'When I die, just throw me in a wheelie bin and they can dump my body on the rubbish tip'.

The eulogy was read by a celebrant provided by the funeral directors. When I asked Mum why she wasn't going to read it, all she said was, 'I wouldn't be able to look my friends in the face if I were to tell barefaced lies in the house of God.'

'But they wouldn't be lies,' I pleaded, 'all you need to do is say a few words about the happy times we had.'

'I don't want people thinking I'm a hypocrite.'

'But...' I began.

'No buts,' she said, firmly, 'and that's my final word on the subject!'

When we arrived at the crematorium, people had already gathered outside. Taking our place behind the coffin, we entered the chapel to the hymn, 'All Things Bright and Beautiful'.

'All things would have been bright and beautiful if it hadn't been for your dad,' said Mum under her breath.

Once everybody was seated, the celebrant took her place at the lectern and introduced herself before saying, 'We are gathered here today to celebrate the life of John Brown...' Then she read some uplifting verses and poems before delivering the eulogy. Once she'd finished, she asked the congregation to spend a little time in quiet contemplation and reflect upon Dad's life.

The curtains slowly began to close as 'Flying Without wings' played in the background. It was only when the coffin disappeared from view that reality finally hit home... I'd never see my dad again. Mum, seeing I was upset, handed me a tissue. We waited until the music was over then slowly left the chapel, closely followed by friends and family.

I was curious to discover who had taken the time to attend the funeral. There were some I knew, some I didn't. Relatives, friends, work colleagues, and neighbours—old and new—all here to pay their last respects. But they weren't the ones who'd caught my attention. There were two characters sitting unobserved in a poorly lit section of the chapel, and I had an uneasy feeling I knew who they were. To confirm my suspicions, while Mum was busy talking, I took the opportunity to sneak back into the chapel and concealed myself behind a tall bookcase. I didn't have long to wait before I heard footsteps. Ducking down, I held my breath and waited. From my hideout, I had a good view of the exit. The vestibule doors opened and out walked Ted and Fergie. Ted stopped next to where I was hiding and, leaning on a shelf, said, 'Let's wait till everyone's gone then we can leave unnoticed. The last thing I want is somebody recognising us.'

'I can't see why we had to come here in the first place, boss. I'm certain the brat got a good look at our phizogs the other week. If she sees us hanging round, she's bound to recognise us. Then she'll start putting two and two together and realise what we're up to,' said a nervous Victor Ferguson.

'I wanted to get a good look at the rest of the family,' said Ted, 'just to get a good idea as to what we're up against. And from what I've so far seen, I don't think we've got much to worry about.'

'If you ask me, the girl and her mum are the ones we need to be watching,' replied Vic, 'if anybody knows anything, they will.'

'Unusually for you, Fergie, I think you're right. If he was going to tell anyone, he'd probably have chosen them. My bet is, they already know where he's stashed the stuff and they're just biding their time, waiting till the heat dies down. Then when they think everybody's forgotten about it, they'll coolly pick up the loot and quietly disappear. And that, Victor my friend, is when we'll be ready and waiting to pounce.'

'The coast's clear now,' whispered Fergie, 'let's go.'

I waited until I was certain they'd finally gone, then I heard Mum frantically shouting, 'Rosie, where are you?'

Covered in dust and cobwebs, I eased myself from behind the bookcase and dusted myself down. Then, as if nothing had happened, I casually walked out of the chapel and into the bright sunlight. 'There you are,' called out Mum, 'where on earth have you been? I've been looking all over the place for you. The limousine's waiting to go.'

'I just popped back to say my last goodbye to Dad.'

She looked me up and down, then said, 'What in God's name's happened to you? You're covered in dust... let me see your hands.'

I held them out then watched in horror as she spat into a tissue and proceeded to wipe my hands and face.

'Mum!' I exclaimed, 'I'm not a baby, everybody's watching.'

'You should have thought about that before you decided to go rolling about on a dirty floor.'

'But I haven't been rolling on the floor!'

'If you haven't, then how come you've got so mucky?'

Unable to answer, I had no option but to grin and bear it.

When she'd finished, she stood back, looked me up and down, and said, 'That's better, now you look more presentable. Hurry up and get in the car, I'm gasping for a cuppa.'

~~~

Mum attended the inquest and listened as the police described the gruesome scene in graphic detail. They said that when his body was found, it was in an advanced state of decomposition. He was still wearing the suit he'd been wearing when last seen and he was holding a briefcase in his hand. By his side they'd found a plastic lunchbox containing a thermos flask, the remains of a ham sandwich and a banana. On the floor next to the body was a partially consumed bottle of whisky and an empty container of Phenobarbitone. The toxicology report stated that they'd found high levels of alcohol and barbiturates in his bloodstream.

The coroner concluded Dad took a lethal cocktail of drugs and alcohol, fell into a deep sleep, then succumbed to hypothermia. The coroners recorded Dad had 'Taken his own life while the balance of his mind was disturbed'.

CHAPTER TEN

I didn't want to be away from school any longer than was necessary. If I stayed at home, I'd only start to brood. In school there was more than enough to occupy my mind.

With the boy's football team temporarily suspended, Mr Preston was able to spend more time coaching the girls. He'd arranged a match for the boys against Horsley Grammar for the following week and was concerned it would have to be cancelled.

When he walked onto the playing field and saw a bunch of schoolgirls trampling over his beloved first team pitch, he looked less than happy. 'Who said you could play on this pitch?' he demanded.

'We thought, as the boys weren't using it, it'd be all right if we did,' I explained.

'You know what thought did, don't you? So, if you don't mind, ladies, can you please make your way to the other pitch?'

'But, we've already put the flags up,' I protested.

'You should have asked me first. Instead, you took it upon yourself to decide which pitch you were going to play on.'

'But it's a cold day and this pitch is much closer to the changing rooms.'

'The top pitch is for the girls, and that's final.'

'That's not fair, sir,' I protested.

'Fair or not, I'm the coach and what I say goes. Now get a move on, it's getting late.'

There was an audible groan from the girls as they trudged round the pitch, pulling up the flags, lugging them up to the top pitch, then setting them up again.

He waited until we'd finished, then shouted, 'Right, girls, separate into two teams and I'll watch while you play. It'll give me a better idea as to where you're up to and whether you've improved since the last time I saw you.' Then, tantalisingly, he said, 'And when you've finished, I've a little surprise for you.'

When we kicked off, every now and again, Mr Preston would shout out instructions, telling us where we should be and what mistakes we were making.

'Brown!' he shouted, 'when you see Morris making a run down the wing, try to time it so you arrive in the box when she's about to put her cross in.'

After the session, Mr Preston shouted, 'Okay, girls, that's all for today. Can you form an orderly line and quietly make your way back into school?'

'But sir,' I shouted, 'you promised us a surprise!'

He stopped. Then in the manner of an absentminded professor who'd forgotten something important, he began to stroke his chin—then his face lit up. 'So I did!' he exclaimed. 'I know you think I spend too much time with the boys, and I have to concede, you may have a point, so I've decided to put things right. You may not have realised it, but I've been watching you closely and I can see you've been working very hard. But if you want to get to the next level, you need to be playing regular games against other teams in your age group. Just playing each other every week isn't going to help, so I've organised a couple of football matches with schools who've also got girls' football teams. Next Friday, I've arranged a game for you against Brentwood School. It's an away match, so I've laid on transport. Unfortunately, I won't be able to go with you, but instead, I've managed to get one of my special friends to accompany you. Some of you may already know her... she plays for Middlechurch United. Any guesses as to who it might be?'

There was a buzz of anticipation as the girls began to speculate as to her identity. 'It'll probably be someone who plays in the reserves,' moaned Jade.

Mr Preston, who was milking it for all it was worth, took a deep breath then announced, 'It's none other than... Jessie Moses!'

Once the cheering died down, he said, 'Before you go, I've got even better news. Not only will she be joining you on the trip, but she's also volunteered to come down every Friday to train you.'

Even though most of us had never heard of her, we let out a loud scream of delight. 'Okay girls, that's it for today. Once you're changed and showered, you can go home.'

Jenny Swift couldn't contain her excitement. 'Somebody pinch me! I can't believe it! Jessie Moses! I'm so excited, I don't think I'll get a wink of sleep till next Friday when I finally get to meet her.'

Not having the remotest idea who she was, I attempted to hide my embarrassing lack of sporting knowledge by meekly replying, 'Me neither.'

When the boys' team was summoned to Mr Critchley's room, he didn't pull his punches, telling them, in no uncertain terms, exactly what he thought of them. 'I've discussed the matter with both the members of staff and the governors. Having examined the evidence, I have concluded that, during a football game between the boys and girls, a serious incident did occur and was aimed at one girl in particular. Before I make my final decision, I'd like to give you the opportunity to explain exactly what brought about this outrageous display of violence.'

Callum stepped forward. 'As team captain, I accept full responsibility for what happened. I've spoken to the rest of the lads and I'm still at a loss to explain why it happened. All I can say is, we're all deeply ashamed. I've spoken to the victim and she has accepted our apologies. In our defence, all I can say is, what happened was totally out of character and we can assure you it will never happen again.'

'Thank you, Callum. I'm reliably informed that what you've just told me is correct. Therefore, I'm prepared to believe this was a one-off occurrence, but I'm still finding it hard to understand why it happened in the first place. Mr Preston has suggested you were expecting to beat the girls quite easily but were taken completely by surprise by their skill and determination. And, not wanting to be humiliated in front of the rest of the school, decided to resort to desperate measures in order to win the game. I'd find it difficult to justify these tactics —even against a team of boys, let alone the girls. Not only was it deplorable, but it was downright cowardly, and you should all be ashamed of yourselves.'

There was a long silence as Mr Critchley reread the report. Then, looking over his glasses, he said, 'I've come to a decision... after much soul searching and following the advice of your form and sports teachers, I've decided to give you one last chance. As from tomorrow, you may resume your sports lessons. But you'll be on probation. And should anything of this nature happen again, I will have no alternative but to subject you to the school disciplinary procedures, which could ultimately result in permanent expulsion from school. I've been very lenient with you today but remember, this is a final warning. I don't want to hear of anything like this happening again. You may resume your lessons.'

Mumbling their thanks, they all trooped out of his office.

~~~

Mum was out when the knock came. I opened the door to find a young police officer carrying a brown cardboard box. 'Is Mrs Brown in?' he enquired.

'No, Mum's out at the moment, but she shouldn't be long.'

'I've come to return Mr Brown's possessions. We've been holding them as evidence, but now the inquest's over, we're returning them to his next of kin.'

'You can leave them with me if you like and I'll give them to Mum when she gets back.'

Frowning, he replied, 'I'm supposed to hand them to his next of kin.'

'Of course. It's up to you, you can wait if you like, but knowing Mum, she'll have bumped into someone and stopped for a chat. So it's anyone's guess what time she'll get back... you could be hanging around for hours!'

I knew this would throw him and felt certain he wouldn't want to waste his time sitting in our front room waiting for Mum's return. That's when I delivered my coup de grâce. 'I'm just as much Dad's next of kin as Mum is, so why don't you leave them with me and I'll give them to her when she gets back... whatever time that is?'

Looking uncomfortable, he shuffled his feet, nervously glanced at his watch, then said, 'Someone's going to have to sign for them.'

'No problem, I'll do it.'

Swiftly snatching his pen, I scribbled my name on the form.

'This is highly irregular,' he protested. Then, resigning himself to the situation, he said, 'Since you're his daughter, I suppose it should be okay.'

Once he'd left, I took the box and placed it on the kitchen table. It was sealed with brown tape and, written in large letters, were the words, 'Police Evidence. Do Not Tamper'.

Should I... shouldn't I? What harm can it do? Mum's gonna be ages yet. So, ripping off the tape, I opened the box then instantly recoiled as a foul smell filled the air. Holding the box at arm's length, I tipped the contents onto the table. There was a watch, a mobile phone, a wedding ring, a wallet, and his lunchbox, alongside various miscellaneous items. It wasn't long before I located the source of the smell. It was a manky, mildew covered briefcase. I was so preoccupied, I didn't hear the key turning in the lock. It was only when the door slammed shut and Mum's voice called out, 'Rosie... I'm home,' that I realised she was back. 'Be a good girl,' she shouted, 'and put the kettle on for your old mum. I'm gasping for a brew.'

I hurriedly stacked Dad's things on top of the briefcase, then balanced it all in one hand while opening the box with the other.

I was hoping I'd be able to put everything back into the carton in one smooth manoeuvre. Not realising how wet and slimy the bag was, as I lifted it, it began to slither and slide on my hand. I made a valiant attempt to prevent the inevitable, but to no avail as everything came crashing to the ground.

Hearing the racket, Mum came flying through the door yelling, 'What on earth's going on in here?' That's when she saw Dad's stuff strewn across the floor. She gave me a suspicious look, then said, 'Where's all that stuff come from?' Before I had time to answer, her sensitive nostrils came to my rescue. Contorting her face, she pinched her nose, held her breath, and gasped, 'What's that bloody awful stench?'

When I explained what had happened, Mum said, sternly, 'The first thing I want is for you to put that dirty old briefcase in the bin. Then when you've washed your hands, you can make me that brew.'

Instead of binning it, I took it to the outhouse and hid it in my secret hidey-hole. When I returned, the kitchen was heavy with the scent of orange blossom. Not only had Mum blitzed the place with air freshener, she'd also put Dad's things back in the box and made two cups of tea. 'What kept you?' she asked. Thinking quickly, I replied. 'I didn't think you'd want it in our bin so I dumped it in next door's.'

'Good thinking, Rosie. Now, let's go into the front room, take the weight off our feet and enjoy a nice cuppa with some dippy biscuits.'

Even though I say so myself, I thought I'd sounded very convincing.

The following day, Mum sorted through Dad's things, separating them into two groups of: DUMP and KEEP. She put his watch and ring in the 'KEEP' section, while his phone and wallet which, to be fair, were in a sorry state, she relegated to 'DUMP'.

'Rosie, could you take this stuff and throw it in the bin please?'

'Okay, Mum. Leave it to me, I'll sort it out.'

There was no way I was going to throw these things away. Apart from my old photos and memories, they were the only things left that had any connection to him. Like a dutiful daughter, I removed them from Mum's sight and secreted them in my wardrobe.

When she'd finished sorting, she said, 'I'll have to pop down to Aldi and get some shopping in. While I'm out, would you give the downstairs a quick Hoover. There's some ready meals in the freezer. Give me half an hour then put the stove on. When it reaches 200°C, pop them in, along with some wedges, and they should be ready by the time I get back.'

As soon as I heard the front door close, I ran to the outhouse, removed the briefcase from its hideout and opened it. Inside was a police evidence bag containing the documents Dad had been carrying with him. From the attached police pro forma, it was obvious they'd made a thorough examination of the contents and failed to find any incriminating evidence. Removing the documents, I put the briefcase back in the hidey-hole, then took them up to my room and hid them in the wardrobe with the rest of his things.

When Mum returned, I said, 'You go and get changed while I put the shopping away. And when you're ready, we'll have our tea.'

'Thanks, love,' said Mum, 'can't wait to flop down in front of the telly, put my feet up and enjoy a nice glass of Prosecco.'

We spent the rest of the evening chatting and watching telly. When it came time for bed, I whispered, 'Goodnight, Mum, I'm off upstairs now.'

'All right, love. Give me a shout when you're ready and I'll bring you up a nice cup of cocoa.'

'Thanks, Mum,' I yawned.

After my cocoa, Mum came in, kissed me goodnight, and switched off the light while I lay in bed listening to her watching 'Celebrity Juice' on the downstairs telly. Knowing she wouldn't budge until the show was over, I switched on the bedside lamp and crept out of bed, making sure to avoid the squeaky floorboard. I then retrieved Dad's things from the wardrobe.

Propped up in bed, I placed them on my beanbag tray, and starting with the wallet, emptied out its contents, Mum having already removed the cash and cards. All that remained were some blotchy photos of me and Mum. If I were to discover anything, the answer had to be hidden among his papers.

I opened the folder and thumbed through the documents. They were mostly financial reports, spreadsheets, unsigned letters, and market forecasts. After the first half dozen, my eyes started to glaze over. What a boring existence, spending Friday night reading through all this grown-up stuff. I was about to call it a day when one document in particular caught my eye. Somehow it seemed different from the rest. The difference was so subtle it was barely noticeable. It was a letter to one of his clients. It read:

Investments Department
Peterson Lange Holdings plc
Bosley House
Riddlestone
Malinshire

Dear Miss Rosebud,
On behalf of Peterson Lange, I would like to thank you for your loyal support during what has been a turbulent year for investors. We are only now beginning to see some light at the

end of the tunnel and believe the time is right to return to the market.

The greatest gains are forecast to be found in the Middle East. A review of your investments indicate you currently hold no Middle Eastern funds in your portfolio.

Fortunately, our Middle East specialist has identified a number of exciting opportunities in his 'Alibaba' class of investments. Of these, fund 'A' seems open, when realigned, to unlock the prospect of lucrative yields. Therefore, I strongly recommend you consider adding this to your investment portfolio.

For further details, please contact me on 08081 575859

Yours faithfully,

John J Brown

Senior Financial Analyst

Peterson Lange Holdings PLC

My eyes widened and the fuzziness cleared as I focused on the contents of the letter. It was addressed to a Miss Rosebud. Rosebud had been Dad's pet name for me. He was forever calling me his little rosebud.

Had he written this letter for me, or was this just an amazing coincidence? Or did he actually have a client called Miss Rosebud? If it were meant for me, then there had to be something very important he wanted me to know. And the clue had to be hidden somewhere in the letter.

It had been a long, tiring day. And although excited by my discovery, there was no way I'd be able to concentrate at that time of night, so I decided to place the mysterious letter in my desk drawer and leave it for another day. I couldn't shake off the feeling Dad was guiding me from beyond the grave—and it sent shivers down my spine.

Jumping back into bed, I immediately fell asleep, only to be rudely awakened by Mum shouting, 'It's Saturday morning!' She then told me I needed to 'get my arse in gear' if I was going to make it on time for my dance class. I dashed about like a scalded cat while Mum made breakfast downstairs. When I came down, I could hear the washer swishing and whirring. She'd already put her uniform on and was busy checking her list of clients for the day.

I gobbled down my porridge and drank my tea. 'Your dance stuff's washed and dried in the airing cupboard. So if you hurry up, I'll drop you off at dance school.'

I shot back upstairs and grabbed my dance gear. I must have had a growth spurt. It seemed like only yesterday I was wearing baggy tights. Now they were stretched to their limit with my big toes threatening to poke holes in them. My leotard wasn't faring any better. What with football, judo and gymnastics, I was rapidly growing out of my sports clothes. Luckily, my dancing shoes still fitted, but it wouldn't be long before they'd also need replacing. I felt sorry for Mum. She badly wanted me to take part in all the activities I'd previously enjoyed.

I hated the thought of her working long hours just to make ends meet. She'd rather starve than ask me to make sacrifices. It was no use, there were decisions to be made and I had to make them. It was all becoming too expensive. At least one of my out of school activities had to go, but which one? If I continued with the dancing, it would mean Mum having to find the money for a whole new outfit. I knew if I continued, Mum would rather deprive herself than see me go without.

It was decision time. After much soul searching, I decided it was time to kick the dance lesson into the long grass. As I already did gymnastics at school, I had a good excuse to scrap that one too, leaving me with judo. The older kids were constantly growing out of their judo outfits so I knew there would always be a supply of cheap secondhand ones. That should save Mum quite a bit of money. My next task was to run it past Mum.

Mum picked me up and as usual, asked my how it'd all gone. 'I didn't really enjoy it today. I think I'm getting too old for dancing, so I've decided it's time I gave it up and concentrated on other things.'

Mum almost blew a gasket. 'Too old for dancing?' she roared, 'you're never too old to dance. What if Fred Astaire had said that when he was a kid?'

'I didn't mean it that way. What I was really trying to say is, I'm involved in too many activities and think it's time I concentrated on the ones I enjoy the most. And unfortunately, dancing isn't one of them.'

'If you give it up now you'll live to regret it. What exactly is it you want to do that's so important?'

'I want to spend more time playing football.'

'There's no future in football, especially for girls, whereas dancing's something you'll be able to do for the rest of your life.'

'That's an old-fashioned attitude. Ladies football's becoming more and more popular. All the big premiership sides have a ladies team.'

'I still think you're making a big mistake. And anyway, I don't see any reason why you can't play football and still dance.'

In reality, I didn't want to give up dancing. If I'd have told her I was only doing it to help her save money, she'd have dug her heels in and made me continue. She can be very stubborn when she wants. I didn't like lying to Mum, but this was an occasion when telling a little white one was the kindest thing to do.

~~~

I was rudely awakened to the chimes of St Paul's church bells. You might think this was quite normal for a Sunday morning, but not in our house. At this time of day, Mum was usually up and about, cleaning and Hoovering. But today, for some reason, it was different. Crossing the landing, I cupped my ear to her door. At first, I couldn't hear anything, then I heard a low moan. I crept downstairs only to find the lounge in disarray. The floor around the sofa was littered with crisps, a wine glass and two empty bottles of Jacob's Creek, part of which had spilled onto the carpet.

I put the kettle on and while I waited for it to boil, I did a quick tidy up. I tried removing the stain, but only succeeded in managing to make things worse. I went back upstairs and tapped on Mum's door. There was no answer, so I knocked again, this time much louder. There was a grunting sound, then a quivering voice croaked, 'Who is it?'

'It's me, Mum. Are you all right?'

'Yes,' she rasped.

'Would you like a cup of tea?'

'I'd love one,' she groaned.

'I'll bring you one up.'

'Can you bring me some paracetamols as well?'

'Yes, Mum. You're not ill, are you?'

'Kind of,' she mumbled.

I made two cups of tea and took one up for Mum. When I entered her room, she was barely visible beneath a mound of bedding. The room was heavy with the sickly smell of whatever Mum had consumed the previous night. Placing her tea on the cabinet, I said, 'There's a bit of a pong in here, Mum. Do you want me to open the window?'

From beneath the duvet, she said, 'Not while they're still ringing those bloody bells.'

Mum must have had a hangover or something, because when she did eventually get up, all she wanted to do was sit around, moaning and groaning while watching rubbish on TV. Whenever I asked her if she'd like something to eat, she'd say, 'I'm not hungry yet, maybe I'll have a sandwich later.' Knowing it had to be a hangover, I put on my coat and, sneaking out of the back door, sprinted down to Mr Sharma's Mini Mart.

'Have you got anything for a hangover?' I asked.

'Rosie,' joked Mr Sharma, 'don't you think you're bit young to have a hangover?'

'It's for Mum, she's a bit under the weather.'

Clutching my box of Alka-Seltzer, I hurried back, managing to creep into the kitchen unnoticed while Mum dozed in the chair. Popping two tablets into a glass of water, I went into the living room and gave her the fizzing drink, 'This is for you, Mum.'

She didn't need telling twice, gulping it down in one. I left her to wallow in her misery while I tidied the kitchen. From out of the living room, came a loud belch, followed by a long silence. Then Mum came bounding into the kitchen. 'I don't know what you put in that drink, Rosie, but I'm already feeling better. I think it's time we made a start on cleaning the house.'

Mum had always enjoyed a glass of wine, especially with a meal, but since Dad died, she'd taken to drinking more often. What started out as a glass of wine on a Saturday night, had turned into several bottles. Although she appeared cheerful on the outside, I knew, deep down inside, she was depressed. She needed something to cheer her up and help take her mind off things, but turning to alcohol wasn't going to help.

CHAPTER ELEVEN

By the time Monday came around, Mum had made a full recovery. Her drinking was a worry, but as it only happened at the weekend, I thought it best not to dwell on it. To be fair, she had a lot on her plate; what with dad's funeral, the electric, gas, and utility bills, not to mention the rising price of food and the cost of keeping a clapped-out motor on the road. How she managed to balance the budget and still have money left over at the end of the month, was nothing short of miraculous. We'd always enjoyed the occasional treat, but over the past few months she'd slowly phased them out, having swapped our regular brands for supermarket's own. What were once Penguins were now Puffins.

Although she'd never like to admit it, I had it on good authority she was using food banks and buying past-their-sell-by-date food. Little did she know, but Milly's Mum had clocked her hanging round the reduced section in Asda, preparing to join in the scrum for the final reductions. So I couldn't really begrudge her her Saturday night treat.

She dropped me at the school gates then checked her watch. Frowning, she rapped the glass of the car's clock, then exclaimed, 'Look at the bloody time ... I should have been at Mrs Eckersley's ten minutes ago. Is there anything in this old shed that works?'

Showering rusty dandruff flakes in all directions, she slammed the door and roared off to see her first client.

The number 27 had just arrived and much to the annoyance of the harassed driver, a rowdy hoard of kids had jammed themselves between the folding doors, each one vying to be first off the bus. Amid the gaggle, I spotted the carrot-topped head of Milly, rucksack draped haphazardly across her shoulder, hair like a frizzy Ayers Rock at sunrise.

'Milly!' I yelled, 'wait for me.'

Hearing my shouts, she waited until I caught up. 'Did you get up to much at the weekend?' I asked.

'Mum went down with the lurgy on Saturday. She was so ill she wasn't able to get out of bed to look after us, so it was left up to muggins here to do everything.'

'Why didn't you get the other two to help?'

'You gotta be joking. They're useless. I made them a list of chores but as soon as my back was turned, they disappeared round to their friends' houses and left me to do it all.'

'It must have been awful. Bet you were knackered.'

'I'll say. By the time seven o'clock came round, I could hardly keep my eyes open. I finally crashed out on the couch next to the dog, but that didn't last long either. I was woken up again by a big sloppy wet tongue on my face. He'd brought his leash from the kitchen so I had to put on some warm clothes and go out in the cold and damp to take him for a walk.'

'What about your mum?'

'She must have overdosed on Night Nurse because, every time I went in to see her, she'd be lying on the bed snoring her head off!'

'How's she today?' I asked.

'She's fine now, but when she woke up on Sunday, she still wasn't too feeling well so she spent the rest of the day on the sofa.'

'And what about the two little layabouts?'

'She must have realised how lazy they'd been because as soon as they were up, she gave them a list of jobs as long as your arm. By the time she'd finished with them, they were in no fit state to do anything else.'

'Serves them right. What did you do?'

'I spent the rest of day just chilling out with Mum.'

I was dying to tell her about Mum's 'illness' but thought better of it. I didn't want anyone to know she'd been drinking. If I'd have described Mum's symptoms, she'd have soon realised she'd been suffering from a hangover.

Changing the subject, I said, 'Milly, you know how the police kept hold of all the stuff they found with Dad's body?'

'Yes?'

'Well, shortly after his funeral they finally decided to release it. Mum sorted through it all, decided most of it was rubbish, then asked me to throw it out. But there was no way I was going to dump it all. Something told me to hang on to it, so instead of binning it, I stashed it all in my secret hidey-hole.'

I went on to tell Milly about the briefcase full of documents and the mysterious letter hidden among them with my Dad's pet name for me written on it. That's when Milly really began to take notice. 'Have you brought it with you?' she asked, excitedly.

'No, I've not had enough time to read through it, but I'm convinced there's something in it Dad wanted me to know— maybe a secret message of some kind.'

'If we put our heads together, Milly, we might just be able to solve the mystery.'

'That'll be great, but I've got to warn you, I'm not very good at solving puzzles.'

'Tell you what I'll do. I'll make some photocopies and let you have one, then you can read it yourself at home. Two heads are better than one and between us we might be able to find out what it is Dad's trying to tell me. But remember, this is just between you and me, even Mum doesn't know about it. So whatever you do, don't let anybody else see it.'

The next day I came to school with a copy for Milly, but before I gave it to her, I made her swear an oath never to show it to anyone else. 'I swear on my mum's life never to tell another soul,' she promised. Her word was good enough for me, so I reached into my bag and gave her a copy.

'This is so exciting,' she said, 'it's just like something from a spy story. All we need now is a gang of villains on our trail, trying to discover our secret.'

I immediately thought of Ted and Fergie and almost blurted it out, but as I still didn't know who they were, or why they'd been watching our house, so I decided not to say anything. I'd given her far too much information as it was, but I knew at some point I'd need help if I were to crack the code.

~~~

For the rest of the week, the talk in school was about the footie match as we counted down the hours and days until Friday. Now it was here, the only thing standing in our way was double maths. I was finding it hard to concentrate, constantly looking out of the window and at the clock, willing the hands towards noon. The sound of Mr Morgan's voice reverberating in my ears soon brought me back to reality. 'Brown!' he roared, 'I don't know what's on your mind today, but it certainly isn't maths. If you want to spend your time staring into space, then maybe you'd like to join my detention class this afternoon, then you'll have all the time in the world to sit and daydream.'

'Sorry, sir. I've not been feeling myself all week and haven't been sleeping properly.'

'I'll overlook it this time,' he replied, 'but from now on, would you please start paying more attention?'

'Yes, Mr Morgan!'

~~~

Jessie was so professional, spending endless hours coaching us. Personally, I thought she was flogging a dead horse. After all, we were just a bunch of misfits. As good as she was, it was going to take a miracle to lick us into shape. But with her never say die attitude, it wasn't long before her enthusiasm began to rub off on us. We were still a bit rough round the edges, but slowly and surely, the genesis of a football team began to emerge. She was like a human dynamo, running up and down the pitch, shouting instructions, pointing out mistakes, showing us areas where we could improve our play. There was still room for improvement, but with our first competitive game just round the corner, we were beginning to feel a little more confident.

Following lunch, we made our way to the locker room and changed into our football kit, ready to board the bus at 12:45.

'Bloody hell,' said Milly, 'it's pouring down.'

'That's okay,' I replied, 'I've got my brolly with me.'

When we arrived at the car park, Mr Preston and Jessie were already waiting by the bus.

'Come on, girls. Get a move on before you get soaked,' shouted Mr Preston.

Huddling under whatever shelter was available, we waited until everybody had assembled. I checked my watch... it was 12:42. 'No sign of Natalie,' whispered Milly, 'I told you she'd bottle it.'

I didn't answer.

Mr Preston, holding a clipboard, shouted, 'Gather round, ladies.'

I looked round, wondering who the heck he was referring to, then the penny dropped. We were the ladies! Obviously he was trying to impress Jessie.

'When you hear your name, please step forward and take your place on the bus.'

One by one, he shouted out our names. When he shouted, 'Natalie Morris!' nobody answered. 'Natalie Morris!' he repeated. Still no answer. 'Has anybody seen Natalie?'

We looked at each other and shook our heads. Mr Preston continued the roll call until everybody was on the bus. When Jessie climbed aboard, the driver closed the door and turned on the engine. He was about to pull away when Mr Preston stepped in front of the bus, furiously waving his arms. The driver jammed on his brakes, stopping the bus with a jolt. Opening the door, the driver shouted angrily, 'Have you got a death wish or something? I could have run you over!' Mr Preston continued gesticulating wildly as he pointed towards the changing rooms.

We all turned to look, and there was Natalie, running headlong towards us. 'You almost missed the bus,' said Mr Preston. 'What kept you?'

'I had a hospital appointment. I thought I'd be back in plenty of time, but one of the doctors didn't turn up so there was a two-hour delay.'

'Quickly, jump on the bus then we can get going.'

Natalie, trying to catch her breath, flopped down next to me and Milly on the back seat. When she was finally able to speak, she gasped, 'Sorry I'm late.'

'We thought you'd bottled out,' said Milly, wryly.

Giving Milly a look of admonishment, I said, 'Some of us might have thought you'd bottled it, but I certainly didn't! I knew there had to be a good reason.'

Once she was able to string together a full sentence, Natalie candidly explained she'd been to the gender reassignment clinic. She wasn't able to tell us the full details but, from the gleam in her eyes, I could see it was potentially exciting news. 'Can't say much more, but when the time's right I'll explain it fully.'

I wasn't sure I wanted to know the full details, but if it was going to help her fulfil her dream, then I was happy for her.

We left the motorway at junction seven and ten minutes later we arrived at Brentwood High. When we alighted, we were greeted by their sports mistress, Mrs Brunch. She shook Jessie's hand and said, 'I'd like to welcome you to Brentwood High, and hope you enjoy your visit.'

As she led us to the changing rooms, I looked over at Natalie. She looked nervous, so I said, 'Don't worry, nobody's going to notice, especially as we're already wearing our football kit.'

'I'm not worried about going on the pitch, it's just... well, it's a bit muddy.'

'What's wrong with a bit of mud?' asked Milly.

'It's not the mud I'm worried about, it's just... they may start wondering why I'm not joining the rest of the girls in the showers.'

'We'll cross that hurdle when we come to it,' I replied, 'I'm sure we'll think of something. If we're stuck, we can always use the old excuse about it being that time of the month!'

Natalie's face lit up. She obviously liked the idea of her having a time of the month.

We ran onto the pitch. There was a strong wind blowing. I had to admit, I had butterflies in my stomach and was starting to wonder what I'd gotten us into, but it was too late for regrets. Here we were, eleven useless girls facing a very experienced football team. Once on the pitch, there'd be nowhere to hide. This would tell us how good we were. If we could keep the score down to a respectable level, we'd be able to hold our heads up high.

With arms round shoulders, we formed a circle around Jessie. 'Okay, girls, this is it, your first competitive football game. Brentwood is a good side. They've been together for a long time and know how each other plays. Whatever happens, if they score first, don't let your heads drop. The last thing I want is for you to get disheartened. All I ask is for you to try your best, and most importantly of all—enjoy yourselves!'

We gave a big cheer then took up our positions.

The referee asked, 'For the pitch side, heads or tails?'

'Tails,' I replied,

She flipped the coin, 'Tails it is. Which end do you want?'

After a quick word, I pointed upwind.

'Okay, Brentwood. When I blow the whistle, you can kick off. And best of luck to both teams.'

The Brentwood captain tapped the ball then passed it back to her midfield. A shiver ran down my spine. This is what we'd been waiting for. We were off.

The game started well. Jade, Tiffany and Ashley were midfield dynamos. Unfortunately, our play was very predictable, making it far too easy for their experienced centre-backs. It was obvious changes were needed. Just when it looked like we'd be going into the break on level terms, disaster struck! Tiffany, who'd been a tower of strength in mid-field, uncharacteristically slipped in the mud, allowing their centre-forward to break through. The Biggs had been in imperious form at the heart of our defence. What they lacked in technical ability, they more than made up for in dogged determination. Surely they'd be able to halt her charge on goal. But this time she was too smart for them. With a swerve and a swivel, she was through. Rhiannon raced across in a forlorn attempt to stop her, only to watch in disbelief as the ball sailed past Milly's outstretched hands.

When the half-time whistle blew, Jessie sprinted onto the pitch. She could see our heads had dropped. 'Come on, girls, why are you looking so deflated? You'd think we'd just lost the FA cup. It's half time and we're only one-nil down, so there's everything to play for. Up until they scored that fluky goal, we'd been far and away the best team. All that's needed is a change of tactics. We've been too predictable; we need to start spreading the ball about and start using our speed down the flanks. If we can supply Natalie and Jennie with enough ball, we'll be able to split their defence and cause them problems at the back for Rosie and Tiff to exploit. Then it'll only be a matter of time before we score.'

We kicked off and straight away our change of tactics began to reap rewards. We were constantly putting their defence under pressure. But luck wasn't with us. No matter how hard we tried, we couldn't turn territorial advantage into goals. With only minutes remaining, Milly collected a weak Brentwood shot and fed it to Rhiannon at right back. She immediately sent Natalie on a sizzling run down the wing before cooly floating the ball into the box, where Tiff was ready and waiting to nod it past their hapless goalie. From the restart, we pressed hard for the winner, only to be thwarted by the shrill of the final whistle.

Thanks to Jessie's coaching, we were fast becoming a formidable unit for our age. Through her footballing contacts, she was able to organise regular fixtures against other schools in our area. We were rapidly gaining a reputation as a difficult team to beat.

At the end of one of our training sessions, Jessie shouted, 'Okay, girls, gather round.'

Forming a semicircle, we stood and wondered what it was she wanted to tell us.

'I'd just like to congratulate you on the progress you've made during the past few months.'

'It's all been down to you!' shouted one of the girls. Then I joined in with, 'Three cheers for Jessie. Hip, hip, hooray.'

Jessie, raising her hand for silence, said, 'Thanks for the support, girls. When we first met, I watched you play and thought, What on earth have I let myself in for? But to your credit, you've managed to prove me wrong. You've improved to such an extent that I now think you're ready to move onto the next level. Therefore, I've decided to enter you in a football tournament. You'll be playing teams of your own age. It's being staged in Marchester. Last week I heard through the grapevine that one of the teams had pulled out and they were desperately looking for another team to replace them. I didn't have to think twice and entered you straight away. It's being played two weeks next Sunday. I know it's short notice, but if you're all happy, and your parents and guardians agree, then it's all systems go.'

We looked at each other in silent disbelief. It took a little time for the news to sink in, but once it had, we answered with one loud voice ... Y-E-S!

CHAPTER TWELVE

Sunday morning, 8.00 am, and for once, everyone was on time. We took our places on the bus and patiently waited while Jessie walked up and down the aisle, clipboard in hand, making her last headcount. Finally satisfied, she signalled the driver to whisk us away. Giving our parents one last wave, we left the car park and headed for our first ever football tournament, singing, 'Here we go, here we go, here we go.'

Listening to their happy chatter as they looked forward to the tournament, I thought to myself, was it only five months ago when I had the crazy notion of forming a girls' football team?

What started out as a bunch of clueless schoolgirls aimlessly kicking a football round the field—much to the chagrin of Mr Preston—had slowly evolved into a well-drilled, well-organised football team. It was one which, in my humble opinion, was able to compete with any team in our age group; and it was all down to one person—Jessie Moses. During the time she'd been with us, she'd managed to work miracles, coaching, cajoling and motivating us until the genesis of a football team finally began to emerge.

All I could do was sit and admire her as she sat, perched next to the driver, tracksuit on, clipboard in hand, planning how we were going to win the tournament. Gazing round, I saw Milly reading her magazine. She'd started as a gangly, overweight girl who couldn't run to save her life. But Jessie saw her potential as a goalkeeper and worked hard on her fitness and skills until she'd made the position her own.

You could've knocked me down with a feather the day Beryl and Brenda Biggs rolled up and asked to join our team. It must have been difficult for them to overcome their shyness. They were always together in school and didn't have any other friends. Whenever they spoke, it only ever amounted to a series of mumbles and grunts. It was rumoured they were the result of an incestuous relationship, but I refused to listen to such idle gossip. I'd also heard they'd been in and out of care for most of their lives and it was this that had made them withdrawn and introverted. Their lack of social skills, combined with the malicious rumours, led everybody to assume they were retarded. They were unusually tall for their age and, as my mum would say, they were 'built like brick toilets'. With their heads down and faces hidden behind their pudding basin haircuts, they'd gained the unflattering nickname of 'The Piltdown Twins'.

Jessie realised their size and presence would be an asset to the team and positioned them at the heart of our defence. Over the months, I'd watched them change from morose introverts to happy confident girls, laughing and joking with the rest of their teammates.

For some reason, the twins had decided to take Natalie under their wing. Maybe it was a case of opposites attract, who knows? With their family background and menacing appearance, they'd acquired a fearsome reputation in the school, and everybody avoided them. If only they'd taken the time to get to know them, then they'd have discovered they were two of the nicest girls you could ever wish to meet.

Jessie hadn't explained the structure of the tournament. The only thing we knew was, we'd be playing in a series of knockout games with the chance of winning our first ever trophy at the end.

The bus's PA system crackled into life and Jessie, tapping the microphone, said, 'Can you hear me at the back?' to the inevitable shouts of, 'No' followed by howls of girlish giggles.

Undaunted, Jessie continued, 'We've just reached the outskirts of town and will soon be arriving at our venue. I'm informed there's likely to be a shortage of changing room space, so I suggest you're all changed and ready by the time we arrive. If there's anyone who wants to change in private, can they remain on the bus until everyone else has left?'

Knowing exactly who she was referring to, we swiftly decamped the bus, leaving Natalie to change in private while the Piltdown's kept guard at the door.

By the time we arrived, the draw had already been made:

James Crawley Academy	v	Goldbourne Grammar
Balcombe Girls	v	Smithfield Girls
Netherton College	v	Avisford High
Hampden College	v	Cullendale College

Cullendale, who had won the trophy for the past two years, were hot favourites to make it a hat-trick. Having never played tournament football before, we were something of an unknown quantity and, as last-minute replacements, we were seen as no-hopers who'd only been included to make up the numbers.

Round One

We were first out of the hat and drawn to play against Goldbourne Grammar. They had a good record in the tournament, having won it three years earlier. Jessie gave us our final team talk before sending us onto the pitch.

'Okay, girls, we're rank outsiders and expected to lose. Personally, I love being the underdog. They'll be expecting a walk in the park, so it's up to us to prove them wrong. We need to be in their faces from the start, harassing them and breaking up their attacks. If they've not scored by half time, they'll start getting frustrated and make mistakes. That's when we can hit them on the break. Rosie, you stay as far up field as you can. Milly, whenever you receive the ball, kick it to either Jennie or Natalie's wing. Jen and Nat, I want you to try and keep possession until Tiff and Rosie are in the box, then you can get behind their defence and with a bit of luck, it'll be goal time!'

The game went exactly as Jessie predicted. Midway through the second half, panic had set in. They were becoming more and more frustrated, passes going astray, heads dropping. With five minutes remaining, their right back attempted a long ball to their centre forward. It was nowhere near strong enough and was intercepted by Ashely Jones, who sprinted through the midfield and eluded two defenders, before sending the most delicate of passes to Tiff, who'd ghosted into the goal area. With only the goalie to beat, she fired the ball into the top, left-hand corner. You could see by their body language they were totally deflated. They spent the rest of the game making mistakes and arguing among themselves until the referee's whistle finally put them out of their misery.

We went wild, jumping, hugging and kissing each other until Jessie brought us back to earth. 'Okay, girls. Calm down, this is only the first round. There's a long way to go. It looks like we'll be playing Smithfield in the next round. If anybody's picked up an injury, however slight, tell me now and I'll put you through your paces to assess your fitness. We can't afford to carry any passengers.'

Semi-Final

Smithfield, like us, was also an unknown quantity. Jessie stressed we shouldn't take them lightly as they'd beaten the highly rated Balcombe in the previous round, albeit by a single goal. Jessie gathered everyone round, read out her team selection, then gave the team talk.

She'd spotted a few areas of our game she believed needed to be tightened up and the tactics to adopt. She'd also sent Rachel Birch to watch their previous game and report back. Although we'd performed well in our first game, she thought we'd played rather negatively. We'd also picked up a couple of niggling injuries, so she decided to rest a couple of players and give the girls on the bench the opportunity to play for their places.

Smithfield, having won the toss, chose to play with the wind. Rachel's report had identified the goalkeeper and their centre forward as their best players and didn't think there was anything special about the rest of the team. Playing into a strong wind, we knew we were in for a torrid first half. We realised that if we could hold out until half time without conceding, we'd have a better chance in the second half. As predicted, they made good use of the wind, lofting high balls into our half. The conditions meant we had to keep the ball low and employ short passes if we were to make ground.

Every member of our team was outstanding in defence, but battling against a strong wind was taking its toll. Constantly having to play in our own half meant we couldn't afford to make mistakes. Half time was looming, and we still hadn't conceded, but we couldn't afford to relax. We'd managed to soak up everything they'd thrown at us; all we were waiting for was the referee's whistle. That's when everything went pear shaped. Beryl, solid as ever in defence, stole the ball from their centre forward and passed it back to Milly. All she needed to do was pass it to Brenda. But for some reason, she had a sudden rush of blood and, inexplicably, she lofted it high into the air only to watch in horror as a freak gust of wind caught hold of the ball, sending it spinning over her head and into our net. 1-0 to Smithfield. Despite our sympathy, Milly was inconsolable, believing she'd let the team down.

At the break, Jessie said, 'They kept us pegged down in the first half, yet they've only got one goal to show for it. The wind's dying down now, so we won't have the same advantage, but from what I've seen so far, I can't see them posing much of a threat. If we keep pressing, I'm certain the floodgates will open.'

Determined to make amends for Milly's mistake, we were quickly out of the blocks, attacking every time we got possession. It wasn't long before we'd taken the lead with two quick goals. Now we could sit back and soak up their insipid attack. With five minutes remaining and hardly a shot on goal,

Milly collected a weak effort from their centre forward and hoisted a towering ball towards Natalie. Tiff and I broke forward to give her support, but I could see she was on a mission. I kept screaming, 'Cross it' but she wasn't listening. Instead, she continued her run until she reached the edge of the area.

The goalie, expecting her to send in a cross, was poised, ready to pluck it out of the air. Instead, from the narrowest of angles, she fired an unstoppable shot between the goalie and the near post. What a goal! The whole team went wild, mobbing Natalie, knowing her wonder goal had put us into the final.

The Final

Apart from a few cuts and bruises, we'd managed to survive the previous games relatively unscathed. This left Jessie with a full squad to pick from, only needing to make a few tactical changes to our lineup. When the officials gave the signal, we ran onto the park and waited for Cullendale to take to the field. When they came out, I was surprised to see that two of their players appeared closer to adulthood than pubescence. Shaking hands with their captain, we exchanged pendants, then pointing to the 'girls', I jokingly said, 'Looks like a couple of your players have had a growth spurt!'

'If it's Tracy and Heidi you're referring to,' she said, snootily, 'they probably have.' She then added, threateningly, 'I hope you've all had your Weetabix today, cos you're certainly gonna need it!'

Taking our positions, we waited for the referee's signal, then we kicked off. Cullendale quickly got into their stride. Tracy and Heidi soon took control of the midfield, bossing the game and giving our girls the runaround. In the background, I could hear Jessie shouting. A swift glance in her direction told me all wasn't well. I could see her gesticulating wildly as she remonstrated with one of the officials. In no time at all, we were 4-0 down and desperately praying for the half-time whistle.

Totally dejected, we trooped off the pitch to find ourselves in the middle of a furious row. 'Those two midfielders are obviously over age,' raged Jessie, 'they've got to be at least seventeen.'

'If you'd have read the rules properly,' countered the official, 'you'd have known that each team is allowed to field two overage players.'

'There's over age and there's those two,' she roared. 'There's no way in the world they're schoolgirls.'

'We only brought in the rule this year, but someone forgot to set an age limit,' he continued, 'so unfortunately they're eligible to play.'

Jessie was steaming when she returned, 'Okay, girls, if that's how they want it, we'll fight fire with fire. Tiff? I'm sorry, but I'm going to have to take you off.'

I looked at our bench and, no disrespect to them, I couldn't see anybody good enough to take her place. I knew we were on the end of a good hiding, but I couldn't see how replacing Tiff was going to improve things. Surely Jessie had lost the plot!

'Jessie!' I pleaded, 'you can't take Tiff off, she's one of our best players. If she doesn't play, we might as well throw in the towel and go home!'

Refusing to listen, she told us to get ready for the second half. Then, to our surprise, she removed her tracksuit, put on her boots and joined us on the pitch.

'Jessie, why didn't you tell us?'

'I decided it was time the gloves came off,' said Jessie. 'If they think it's fair to play adults against children then, from here on in, it's no holds barred.'

As soon as they kicked off, Tracy and Heidi received the ball and, as they'd previously done, they tried using their strength and speed to boss the midfield. It was obvious they'd never heard of Jessie. Tracy picked up the ball and tried dribbling past her but was quickly brought down to earth when Jessie skilfully picked her pocket, leaving her wondering what had happened. Leading by example, she was barking out her orders while splitting their defence with her accurate passes. I could feel the gloom begin to lift as we watched Jessie in full flow. Once Cullendale had lost control of the midfield, Jessie was unremitting, putting their defence under constant pressure. It was only a matter of time before they cracked.

They'd never faced anybody like Jessie before and were totally mesmerised by her skills. Her presence on the pitch was inspirational. Suddenly, we had a spring in our step. Once we became accustomed to her pace, we were able to feed off her inch perfect passes and started to punch holes in their defence. The first half had been a nightmare; now we were in dreamland. With our tails up, there was no stopping us. It wasn't long before Natalie collected one of Jessie's pinpoint passes and sprinted down the wing. Just before she reached the byline, she floated a tantalising cross, just beyond the reach of the goalie, to where I was waiting, ready to slot it into the back of the net. After that goal, we managed to score three more to draw level. With only ten minutes remaining, both teams were tiring, and it began to look increasingly likely that whoever scored the next goal would win the game, and with it, the tournament.

Cullendale's coach went frantic. She ran up and down the line, screaming at the top of her voice, trying everything she could to lift her deflated team and urge them forward for one last attack —but our defenders stuck to their task. Beryl intercepted a through ball and casually tapped it back to Milly, who immediately hoisted it upfield towards Jessie. The sight of Jessie in full flow with the ball at her feet sent their coach into a blind panic. 'Stop her!' she screamed.

The only players ahead of her were Tracy and Heidi. Since she'd come on, Jessie had outplayed and humiliated them. Now they saw their chance to exact their revenge. Jessie, fully aware of their intentions, didn't even attempt to avoid them.

She waited until they were within tackling distance then watched as Tracy, studs up, launched herself at her ankles while Heidi closed in to finish the job. Jessie was far too clever for that. As cool as a cucumber, she nutmegged Heidi, then leaped clear of the incoming tackle, leaving Tracy sliding helplessly across the greasy pitch before connecting with Heidi's ankle. There was a sharp crack and a harrowing scream as Heidi lay on the pitch writhing in agony. Meanwhile, Natalie, who'd ghosted in from the wing, collected the ball, dummied the goalie and popped it into the back of an empty net. 4-5 to James Crawley.

Tracy was immediately shown the red card while Heidi was stretchered off and taken to hospital with a suspected broken leg. With her job done, Jessie left the field to be replaced by Alisha Dobson. Without Tracy and Heidi, Cullendale looked less than ordinary, never managing a single shot on goal. When the final whistle blew, we all collapsed, exhausted, onto the ground. Thanks to Jessie, we'd snatched what seemed like an unlikely victory from the jaws of defeat.

After the game, both sides posed for team photographs then lined up for the presentation ceremony.

We wanted Jessie to accept the trophy on our behalf, but she bluntly refused, saying, 'It's the captain's job to receive the trophy, not mine.'

The PA system crackled into life. 'Commiserations and a big hand to the gallant losers... Cullendale!'

From behind, somebody booed. I looked around and saw the guilty-looking face of Milly.

Underjoyed, the less than gallant losers took it in turns to receive their medals, refusing to shake hands as they filed past us. Excited, we waited for our big moment. When the MC declared, 'A round of applause for the winners of our trophy... The James Crawley Academy!' we let out a loud cheer.

I led the team to where the mayor was waiting. Shaking my hand, he congratulated me on our victory then presented me with the trophy. I proudly held it aloft to the applause of a small, but appreciative audience as the rest of the team followed closely behind, having just collected their medals.

Facing the long journey home, we quickly showered and changed, then hurried back to the bus. We were about to leave when an announcement came over the tannoy, 'Finally, the presentation for the player of the tournament.'

'Player of the tournament!' exclaimed, Milly, 'I didn't even know they were having one.'

'Neither did I,' said, Jessie. 'Looks like we'll have to have to hang around a little bit longer.'

We trooped off the bus and gathered by the podium to await the judges' decision.

There was a long pause... then the announcer declared, 'It's been a great tournament, and there have been some outstanding performances but, after much deliberation, the judges have decided the player of the tournament is—Natalie Morris!'

'Well done, Natalie, you deserve it,' said Jessie. Then, adding a note of urgency, she said, 'We need to get a move on if we're going to get back on time.'

It had been a long, tiring day and once back on the bus, we all collapsed in our seats, tired, exhausted, aching, and happy. One thing was certain, we'd played our hearts out. We'd certainly sleep tonight, but would we be fit enough for school in the morning?

CHAPTER THIRTEEN

It was a cold, dank, murky evening when we finally arrived at school. The amber glow of the streetlights struggled to illuminate the car park as parents, guardians and caregivers slowly emerged from whatever shelter they'd managed to find. But what did we care? All we wanted was to celebrate our victory. Waiting patiently until everybody was safely off the bus, a weary Jessie gave the driver the thumbs up before the bus disappeared into the early evening gloom.

'Hurry up and get in the car,' shouted an angry mum, 'I'm getting soaked!'

With the trophy safely tucked up in my sports bag, I made a dash for the car. I was about to place it on the back seat when Mum growled, 'Don't even think of putting that stinking bag on the car seat. Put it in the boot.'

'But the trophy's in here, it might get damaged in the boot.'

'Less of your guff and do as you're told, m'lady.'

I could tell by the tone of her voice she was in a bad mood, so I thought it best not to argue.

With a face like thunder, Mum slammed the boot shut then settled herself behind the steering wheel while I sat in the passenger seat next to her.

Hoping she'd calmed down, I dangled my medal in front of her and said, 'Aren't you going to congratulate me?'

'Congratulate you?' she roared, 'Congratulate you... that's a good one. You keep me hanging round for over two hours then you want me to congratulate you?'

'It wasn't our fault. They made us wait until the player of the tournament was announced—and you'll never guess who won it?'

'I couldn't give a toss who won it. It's getting late and you've got to be up for school in the morning, so less of your yatter and let's get going.'

'It was Natalie,' I persisted... 'Our Natalie!'

'Hmm,' she grunted disapprovingly. 'Why you can't play a nice, sensible game like netball is beyond me.'

I didn't even bother replying. I mean... what was the point?

She buckled her seatbelt, inserted the key into the ignition and, taking a deep breath, prepared herself for her ongoing battle with the car. But to everyone's surprise, and offering minimal resistance, it roared into life.

With a wry smile, she licked her finger and made an imaginary mark on an invisible scoreboard, then exclaimed, 'One up for me, I think.' Not wanting to tempt fate, she pressed hard on the accelerator and kept it there until she was absolutely certain it hadn't been toying with her and was about to cut out. Once satisfied, she switched on the headlights, picking out Beryl and Brenda as they trudged, heads down, out of the school gates. Wearing only thin nylon anoraks, they were leaning into the stiff breeze as they battled against the elements.

'Mum!' I shouted, pointing towards the twins, 'See those girls over there? I don't think anybody's coming to meet them.'

Mum frowned as she looked at the bedraggled pair. 'No wonder. They look as if they've just escaped from prison.'

'Mum, they've just helped us win a football tournament.'

'I still think they look like a pair of criminals.'

'Mum, they're really nice girls once you get to know them.'

'That's as maybe, but I wouldn't like to bump into them in a dark alley.'

'I don't care what you think. All I know is, they're too young to be walking the streets at night. The least we can do is offer them a lift... Mum... please...?'

'All right, if you really want me to, but I can't say I'm happy about it.'

While I was fastening my seatbelt, Mum slowly drove past the twins then stopped slightly ahead of them. As they were about to pass, she opened her window and called out, 'Can we give you a lift?'

They looked inside to see who was sitting in the passenger seat. When they saw who it was, Beryl said, 'It's all right, Mrs Brown, there's a bus stop just round the corner.'

'It's a Sunday service,' replied Mum, 'the last bus went ages ago.'

Brenda whispered something in Beryl's ear, then Beryl said, 'We live at the bottom of Blackstone Lane, it's on the outskirts of town, just off Dutton Road, if that's not taking you too far out of the way?'

'Throw your stuff in the boot and jump in,' replied Mum.

Throughout the journey, Mum tried making small talk, you know, the way mums tend to do, but every time she asked them about their background, they'd clam up.

Soon, we'd left the town and were on the road to Dutton. There was a fine drizzle and the road was poorly lit. To see where she was going, Mum put the headlights on full beam. A voice from the back called out, 'Blackstone Lane's just round the next bend on the left, Mrs Brown.'

With her wipers on full speed to ensure she wouldn't miss the turn, Mum slowed down to a crawl. Her headlights picked out a barely distinguishable sign pointing towards a narrow lane. She wound down the window, popped out her head and read, 'Blackstone Lane'.

We turned onto an unlit road, passing a disused farm on the left and open fields on the right. We continued until the headlights picked out a tall, corrugated fence. 'Just before that scrapyard,' shouted Beryl, 'there's a concealed entrance. If you drive down to the end of the track, that's where we live.'

'Ooh,' said Mum, sounding impressed, 'I didn't realise you lived on a farm.'

'Technically you could call it a farm,' said Brenda, vaguely.

At the end of the lane was a five-barred gate, behind which caravans, trucks, cars, and construction vehicles were parked. Our arrival was heralded by the sound of barking dogs.

When we reached the entrance, there was a reception committee waiting, our headlights only serving to accentuate their size. A large, swarthy man stepped forward. He had a weather-beaten face and wore a brown trilby over his dark wavy hair. He sported a red polka dot neckerchief, hobnail boots, brown corduroys, a grubby white vest, and a leather waistcoat. Trying not to sound frightened, Mum said, 'He must be frozen solid dressed like that.'

Holding up his hand, he indicated to Mum to switch off the engine. He walked up to the driver's side then signalled for Mum to wind down the window. 'What are you wanting round here?' he demanded. Before she could answer, Beryl shouted from the back, 'It's only us, Uncle Paddy.'

Relaxing his aggressive stance, he smiled and said, 'It's okay, lads, it's only the girls back from their football match.'

Mum helped them out of the car and retrieved their bags from the boot, then accompanied them to the gate. 'How did you get on?' asked Paddy?

Holding up their medals, they said, 'We won!'

Paddy ushered them through the gate and slammed it behind him, then said, grumpily, 'Thanks missus. You can go now.'

Mum clung onto the gate hoping to get a better view of the camp, but they closed ranks, forming an impenetrable barrier. Paddy, who was quickly losing patience, growled, 'I said you can go now, missus!'

Mum, getting scared, climbed into the car, did a quick reverse then, tyres screeching, sped down the track. It was only when we were safely on the road into town that she spoke.

'They're not very friendly, are they? I'll bet you a pound to a pinch of salt they've got something to hide. And while we're on the subject, why didn't you tell me they were gypos?'

'I've only just found out myself... and stop calling them gypos!'

'I ought to have known,' she continued.

'And why's that?'

'Because of the way they look.'

'But it was only a few minutes ago when you thought they were farmers' daughters.'

'Only because they told me they lived on a farm! If I'd known, I'd never have given them a lift.'

'Mum, they're travellers, not criminals!'

'They didn't make me very welcome!'

'They suffer a lot of discrimination, that's why they're suspicious of strangers.'

'They're still gypos as far as I'm concerned. I wouldn't trust them as far as I could throw them. In fact, I wouldn't be surprised to find our wheel trims missing when we get home.'

~~~

Helga Schmidt paced the goalmouth like a caged tiger, using every trick in the book to distract me. There was no way on earth she was going to stop me from scoring the goal which would take us into the European Cup Final. Fixing her with a cold, hard stare, I started my run then, feigning part way, sent her diving in the wrong direction. With the goal at my mercy, victory was assured. Suddenly, an ear-splitting sound filled the air, breaking my concentration. Mis-hitting the ball, I ballooned it over the cross bar. In a fit of anger and frustration, I lashed out, sending the culprit crashing to the ground... but still the noise continued... It's no use, I'm going to have to get up and stop it!

Throwing back the covers, I leapt out of bed. That's when it hit me! Emitting a piercing scream, I collapsed onto the mattress, barely able to move. The pain was excruciating. Every bone in my body ached. Convinced I'd lost the use of my limbs, I cried out, 'Mum, come quick, I've been struck down by some kind of illness!'

Bursting through the door, she picked up the alarm clock, silenced it and said, 'What's all the commotion?'

'Every time I try to move, I'm in pain.'

'It's your muscles, they're aching from yesterday's football.'

'I can't go to school like this.'

'Of course, you can, a nice hot bath will soon put you right.'

When I entered the bathroom, the smelt of herbs and eucalyptus was overpowering. I gently eased myself into the bath and relaxed, letting the water soothe away my aches and pains. Feeling refreshed, I dressed and came down to find Mum busy making a fry up. 'Sit down and I'll bring you your breakfast.'

A fry up is something of a rarity in our house, normally we eat on the go. 'What's the occasion?' I asked.

'You didn't have very much to eat yesterday, so I thought it'd be a good idea to give you a full English.'

I had to admit, I was ravenous, playing so much football in one day had taken it out of me.

'Can I have a little look at your trophy before you take it into school?' asked Mum.

Taking it out of my bag, I handed it to her. 'Wash your hands first,' I said, 'I don't want bacon fat all over it.'

Following my rebuke, she washed her hands then carefully held it in the air. 'I'm sorry I didn't show any interest in your achievement yesterday. I was in a bad mood.'

'Don't I know it! After your long wait, it's understandable.'

'I'd just like to say, I'm very proud of you, Rosie. Your team must have played really well to win this.'

With Mum grumpy and me tired, I'd not had the chance to tell her about our amazing win, but once I got started there was no stopping me. I was still raving about it when she dropped me at the school gates. Heading straight for Mr Critchley's office, I reluctantly handed it to Mrs Burrows.

'Could you make sure Mr Critchley gets this trophy before assembly, Mrs Burrows?'

'Is this the one you won yesterday?'

'Yes, it is,' I replied.

'You should all be proud of yourselves, it's a wonderful achievement.'

At assembly, Mr Critchley came onto the stage carrying the trophy then asked the team to join him. 'I don't know if everybody's heard yet,' he announced, 'but our girls' team played in their first ever football tournament yesterday and against all the odds, they won this magnificent trophy!'

Reluctantly, my teammates pushed me to the front. Mr Critchley handed me the trophy and I lifted it above my head, upon which the whole room erupted.

Following the assembly, I accompanied Mr Preston to the main entrance, where the trophy was given pride of place in the trophy cabinet.

The rest of the week was a bit of an anticlimax. Having been on cloud nine, it was now back to reality.

On Thursday afternoon, Mr Preston popped his head through the gym door and beckoned to Miss Meadows. After a quick word, she came over to me and said, 'Can you get changed and accompany Mr Preston to Mr Critchley's office please?'

'What's it all about, sir?' I nervously asked as we walked down the corridor.

'Don't worry, you've done nothing wrong, it's just that ... something's cropped up and the head wants to discuss it with you.'

I knocked, then entered. The head was standing next to a smartly dressed man in a white shirt, grey trousers, regimental tie, and a blazer with three lions emblazoned on the breast pocket. 'Rosie,' said Mr Critchley, 'I'd like to introduce you to Andrew Grizedale, he's chair of the county football association. He's here to investigate claims we used an ineligible player during Sunday's tournament.'

Thinking it was Jessie he was referring to, I immediately went on the offensive and said, 'Jessie only played for a short time, and only because Cullendale cheated by bending the rules.'

'Whoa, slow down young lady,' said Mr Grizedale, 'who mentioned Jessie?'

'Mr Critchley,' I replied indignantly, 'he said we played an ineligible player!'

'Yes, and so he did, but the complaint's got nothing to do with Jessie.' Looking uncomfortable, he started tugging at his shirt collar, hesitated, cleared his throat, then continued, 'It's a rather delicate issue concerning the gender of one of your players.'

I instantly knew what he was talking about. With hackles raised, I prepared to launch myself into a strident defence of Natalie, when Mr Critchley stepped in, saying, 'If it's Natalie Morris you're talking about, then as far as the school's concerned, she's a girl, and as such, fully entitled to play in the team.'

'That's as maybe,' replied Mr Grizedale, 'but strictly speaking, anatomically she's male and the rules of the competition state that only females are allowed to play.'

I tried arguing but he wouldn't listen.

'Rules are rules I'm afraid, so as far as the FA is concerned, Natalie Morris is a boy and as such was ineligible to play.'

Rising to leave, he said, 'I'll be submitting a report based on my findings, but I can tell you now, it's not looking good.'

~~~

How they got hold of the story I'll never know, but the very next day it had made the front page of the local newspaper. And it wasn't long before it had been picked up by the rest of the press. The next thing I knew, we were besieged by reporters all wanting to hear Natalie's side of the story. They even came to my house but were given short shrift by Mum.

By Monday, the story had gone viral. Now the world's press were reporting it. There was no sign of Natalie in school, how could she come with the world and his dog camped outside her house ready to pounce?

Using word of mouth, I secretly organised a meeting for Tuesday lunchtime in the gym—a time I knew when it would be empty.

As I walked through the gymnasium door, a loud cheer went up. I couldn't believe how many people had taken the time to attend. Standing on a bench, I called for silence, then said, 'Listen everybody, we won that trophy fair and square and now they want to take it away from us just because Natalie played in our team. Sometime this week, they'll be coming to take it away, which leaves us with very little time. That's why I've called this meeting. Firstly, we need to form a committee to coordinate any actions that come out of this.'

Sandy Lawson, a sixth form student, stood up and said, 'I'm older than most of you and have been involved in plenty of protests, making me more than qualified for the job. I therefore would like to put myself forward to be the action committee leader. With my experience and contacts, I believe I'd be the ideal candidate.'

'Sounds good to me,' I said. 'Who's in favour of Sandy leading us?'

Every hand in the room went up. 'I think that's unanimous, Sandy.'

I was pleased to see that Sandy was joining us. She'd grown up immersed in politics. Her dad, Jack Lawson, was the leader of the local Labour Party while she was as an active member of the Young Socialists. With Sandy behind us, how could we possibly fail?

Sandy stood next to me and, looking every bit like a radical student leader, shouted, 'I'd like to hear some suggestions, please?'

'Have they taken the trophy yet?' asked Tiffany.

'No,' I answered, 'but they will. Probably sometime this week.'

Someone else asked, 'Why don't we just take it out of the cabinet and hide it?'

'We can't,' I replied. 'Mrs Burrows holds the keys and keeps them locked away in her office.'

'You're the team captain,' he demanded, 'surely they'd allow you to borrow the trophy for a couple of days.'

'If he got wind of what we were up to, Mr Critchley would never allow me to have it.'

There was a roar of approval when a voice from the back shouted, 'Why don't we just break open the cabinet and take it?'

'That would be a criminal offence,' I countered.

'Why don't we have a sit-down protest when they come to take it away?' suggested Milly.

'Well, done, Milly,' I said, 'that's the best idea we'd had so far. What do you think, Sandy?'

'I think it's a brilliant idea,' she replied, 'but if it's going to work, we'll need to get the media involved.'

'Do you think you'll be able to organise it?' I asked.

'I don't see why not! All we need to do is wait until we see them coming then we can spring into action. Now here's my plan...'

Sandy's organisational skills were second to none. With little time to spare, she spent the rest of the day formalising a plan of action as well as organising a team of observers whose job was to monitor the school's comings and goings. If they spotted anybody remotely resembling an FA official, they were to report back to either Sandy or me so one of us could investigate. With preparations in place, all we were waiting for now was the arrival of an FA official.

It was Wednesday afternoon when it finally kicked off. Sandy's team of lookouts was really taking their job seriously, using binoculars to scrutinise everyone who visited the school. As soon as the enemy was located and identified, the word would be passed round to mobilise the students.

One of our lookouts who was watching the main gate, saw a silver Mercedes approaching and immediately messaged Sandy, who in turn alerted me. 'Possible enemy sighting,' she texted, 'about to intercept. If sighting confirmed, will employ delaying tactics until troops can be deployed.'

Sandy, sprinting to the car park, managed to waylay them before they could enter the building.

She saw by the badges on their blazers they were FA officials and gave the signal to go into action.

'Good afternoon,' said Sandy as they were leaving their car. 'I'm Sandra, your school greeter, how can I help?'

'We're from The Football Association...'

'No need to explain,' she interrupted, 'I know exactly why you're here. Please follow me.' She then proceeded to steer them in the opposite direction while she recited the school mission statement:

'We at The James Crawley Academy,' she prattled, 'are committed to providing a learning environment where the priority is to foster a love of learning by building and developing all our individual talents, working tirelessly to ensure our students enjoy a stimulating and diverse educational experience...' Then, barely pausing for breath, she resumed, 'Our vision is to forge strong, positive connections with our students so they can achieve independence, build confidence and gain academic knowledge.'

'Excuse me, young lady, but are you sure we're going in the right direction?'

'Yes,' she replied, 'the playing fields are just down here.'

'I think we may be at cross purposes,' he protested, 'we're here to meet with the school head.'

'I'm terribly sorry,' said Sandy, 'my mistake. When you told me you were from the FA, I automatically assumed you'd come to inspect our sports facilities.' Then, glancing up at the window and seeing the thumbs up sign, she continued, 'I'll take you straight to Mr Critchley's office.'

Meanwhile in school, everyone was leaving their classes and marching towards Mr Critchley's office. Once they arrived, they sat on the floor and began chanting, 'Justice for Natalie.' In the meantime, Sandy was busy contacting her friends in the press and TV, alerting them to our protest.

Hearing the commotion, Mr Critchley rushed out to investigate, closely followed by his two visitors.

'What's the meaning of this?' he roared. 'Return to your classes at once!'

Stepping forward, I said, 'We're not moving until we're reinstated as the tournament winners.'

'I'm sorry, Rosie, but the organisers have decided we broke the rules. Therefore, we've no alternative but to return the trophy.'

That's when the TV reporter burst in. The camera-shy officials, not wanting publicity, made a dash for the door, hotly pursued by the rapidly arriving reporters and cameramen, hiding their faces and refusing to answer any questions. Having achieved our first objective, we victoriously returned to our classes, aware there'd be further battles ahead.

Later that evening, the school was featured on local news bulletins, where footage of our sit-in was shown. I arrived at school the next day to find TV news teams waiting at the gate. As soon as they recognised me, they swarmed around asking for an interview. I knew I'd be breaking school rules but believing I had no other alternative; I accepted their request.

'This is Rosie Brown, captain of the James Crawley girls' football team, which controversially won a football tournament only to be stripped of the title for fielding an ineligible player,' said the interviewer.

'Rosie?' he asked, 'the rules state that it was a girls only tournament yet you chose to flout those rules by playing a boy in your team, so why have you decided to make this protest?'

'The boy you're referring to is actually living her life as a girl, and in our school, she is treated as such. Just because she's in transition, doesn't mean she can't take part in normal sporting activities. She's an integral part of the team and was selected on merit. To deny her a place in the team would have been a breach of her human rights.'

The reporter continued, 'But don't you think she has an unfair advantage over other girls of her age?'

'She's no stronger than the rest of us,' I replied, 'in fact she's one of the smallest girls in the team, so the answer's a definite NO!'

Following my television interview, civil rights and LGBT activists and supporters were soon championing her cause and a mass picket of the FA headquarters was organised. Transgender MP for Bursham south, Jade MacAllister, tabled a commons motion expressing support for Natalie and demanded government intervention.

Ms MacAllister, standing up in parliament, asked, 'You may be aware, Prime Minister, that a girl's football team has recently been stripped of their trophy by The Football Association for fielding a transgender person. Does the prime minister agree that the FA acted unfairly?'

'This was an internal decision made by the board of the English Football Association,' he replied. 'This morning, my sports minister called an urgent meeting with the FA's chief executive officer expressing her unease at the decision. I can now tell the honourable lady that the CEO has taken on board our concerns and has promised to undertake an urgent review of the case. We are hopeful that an amicable solution will soon be found.'

Under intense public and media pressure, the FA finally caved in and reinstated us as winners.

Once the dust had settled, Mr Critchley, who'd been reticent on the subject, called me into his office. 'I've brought you here to express my displeasure at the scenes of ill-discipline displayed in our school and witnessed by the rest of the country on television. Your action, laudable though it may be, was at best ill-conceived and at worst, foolhardy and potentially damaging to the school's reputation.'

'Though I have sympathy with the cause, I am unable to condone your actions. Therefore, I am left with no alternative but to issue you with a written warning. I'd just like to add that if you have any grievances, however trivial, could you please make them through the appropriate channels? Now you may return to your class and think yourselves lucky I've been so lenient.'

Suitably chastened, I walked to the door only to hear Mr Critchley whisper, 'By the way Rosie, Natalie's parents send you their regards and you'll be glad to know that she'll be back in school on Monday.' Then he smiled and said, 'That'll be all, Rosie.'

CHAPTER FOURTEEN

I'd become so preoccupied with the football team and the controversy surrounding our tournament victory that I'd managed to push the arduous task of deciphering Dad's letter to the back of my mind. Now it had all been resolved, there was nothing left to occupy my time, so I decided to make a determined effort to try and solve the mystery of the 'Rosebud' letter.

As I'm easily distracted, I resolved to spend some time in the library and attempt to figure out exactly what Dad was trying to tell me. But first I had to run it past Mum.

'I need to go to the library on Saturday, Mum.'

'What for?'

'To do some research for a history project I'm doing.'

'Why can't you do it here?'

'Because they've got reference books and historical documents, and if I need any help, they've also got an archivist.'

'Surely you can find all that stuff on the internet.'

'Mrs Dean wants us to start using primary source material now we're working towards our exams.'

'What the eye doesn't see, the heart doesn't grieve over!'

'That would be cheating, Mum, and anyway, Mrs Dean can always tell when somebody's been cheating.'

'Then you'd better do as she says, we don't want you getting into trouble. Do you want me to run you there?'

'No thanks, Mum, I'll use my bus pass.'

'Then I'll make you a packed lunch. What do you want on your sandwiches?'

'What have you got?'

She opened the fridge, looked inside, and said, 'It'll have to be either cheese spread, Spam or fish paste?'

Shuddering, I replied, 'It's okay, Mum, I'll get something in town.'

'You're not wasting good money on overpriced sandwiches. You're taking a packed lunch and that's the end of it!'

~~~

Following the Ted and Fergie incident, I'd found myself constantly peeping through curtains, checking to see if they'd returned. Over time, when they hadn't returned, I started to relax. But from what they'd said in the crematorium, I knew they wouldn't give up until they'd found what they were looking for.

This was going to be my first unaccompanied journey since my terrifying encounter with the two thugs, so I was understandably apprehensive. With my copy of the 'Rosebud' letter, a pencil case, notepad, and Mum's dreaded packed lunch, I started out for the library.

Setting myself up in a quiet corner of the reference room, I commenced the laborious task of dissecting the letter, sentence by sentence, word by word. It wasn't until mid-morning before I finally managed to whittle it down to one short sentence:

"Fund 'A' seems open, when realigned, to unlock the prospect of a lucrative yield. Therefore, I strongly recommend you seriously consider Fund 'A' as part of your investment portfolio."

The more I looked at it, the more it became obvious Dad's use of the phrase, 'I strongly recommend' was his way of telling me a message was hidden in the sentence. But it was still all gobbledygook to me. No matter how hard I tried, I just couldn't figure out what it was he was trying to tell me.

A full morning staring at the letter, jotting down notes and staring at a computer screen had finally taken its toll. My eyes were red raw, my head ached, I was spitting feathers, and my belly was starting to think my throat had been cut. It was time to call it a day. The room was hot and clammy, and the sun was streaming through the stained-glass windows. I sat, eyes closed, head cradled in clammy hands, trying to clear my head. Then a voice in my ear said, 'Excuse me, young lady, this is not a dosshouse, you know.'

I looked up to find a stony-faced harridan glaring down at me. With her white blouse, grey skirt, black tights, and hair tied up in a bun, it could only have been one person—the head librarian!

'I'm sorry, Miss, I've been studying hard all morning and now I've ended up with a blinding headache.'

'I've had numerous complaints about a rotten smell emanating from this room,' she sternly replied, 'you wouldn't happen to know about it.'

'To be honest, I haven't smelt a thing, but now as you're mentioning it, there does seem to be a bit of a pong.' Like a leopard stalking its prey, she circled the room, sniffing in every nook and cranny before returning to say, 'The smell appears to be strongest around here.'

Realising Mum's fish paste butties might be the source of the smell, I said, 'It's probably the drains. Why don't you open a window?'

She pointed at my bag then said, accusingly, 'You've not got food in there, have you?'

'No!' I replied.

'You do realise it's prohibited to bring food into the library,' she continued.

'I've not got any food,' I lied.

Hoping to extract a full confession, she fixed me with an accusing stare. Determined not to waver, I held her gaze until, in frustration, she finally blinked and said, 'I'm just off to get a pole to open the top windows; I won't be long.' Then, pinching her nostrils, she sidled out of the room.

Once she'd gone, I grabbed my things and made a swift exit via the revolving doors. With the afternoon to myself, I decided to spend it chilling out in the town centre.

When I arrived, the shops, bars and cafés were buzzing. Everybody must have had the same idea as me and decided to come into town to take advantage of the unseasonably warm weather. With every bench fully occupied, I decided to bide my time and wait until a space became available, but as soon as one did, someone would appear and pounce on it.

There was a man sitting on the end of one of the benches, chewing on the plastic cap of his ball point pen as he wrestled with a crossword puzzle. Doing a rough calculation, I estimated there had to be at least half a 'bum's width' of space remaining. As I'm petite, I walked over to the man and politely asked, 'Is there room for a little one?'

'Of course, there is,' he replied.

Easing myself onto the end, I had a wicked thought, *It's a good job I'm not built like the Biggs*'. Then, immediately regretting it, I mentally reproached myself. I removed my lunchbox and, placing the bag between my legs, I removed the lid. I was immediately hit by the smell of 'well past its best' fish paste which, only hours earlier, had been sandwiched between two slices of bread. The warm conditions in the library hadn't helped and now my butties were almost, but not quite, inedible.

That's when Milly's mum spotted me. 'Milly, look who's over there,' she shrieked, 'it's Rosie!' With everybody on the street looking at me, I didn't know where to put my face.

'Shush Mum,' said Milly, 'you're embarrassing her.'

'It's your friend, Rosie,' she squealed, 'let's join her.'

I could see Milly was equally embarrassed. Her normally red complexion was slowly turning a deep scarlet.

'You sit with Rosie, and I'll go and get you some chips. Do you want any, Rosie?'

Although I could have demolished them, I replied, 'No thanks, Mrs Hampson.'

Unusually for her, Milly was left dumbstruck as she patiently waited for a space to appear. An old lady on the other end was just finishing her sandwiches. Throwing the crusts on the floor, she fastened the flap on her trolley, stood up, brushed the remaining crumbs from her lap, then using her trolley for support, she shuffled off down the street. All of a sudden, a flock of pigeons appeared. There was a flurry of crumbs, claws, beaks, and feathers and the bread disappeared. Then they returned from whence they came.

Milly, deciding to mither Mr Crossword Man, said, 'You couldn't push up a bit could you, mate, so I can sit next to my friend, Rosie?'

'Certainly,' he replied.

Just as Milly sat down, her mum arrived, carrying a huge tray of chips.

'Is it okay if leave you both in peace while I go and have a good old rummage in the charity shops. I'll only be a few minutes.'

'And the rest,' replied Milly.

Angrily, Milly turned to me and said, 'You told me you never come into town on a Saturday cos you're always too busy.'

I decided it was time I laid my cards on the table. So, taking a swig from my bottle of pop, I told her everything—the dream, Fergie and Ted, the chase, the funeral. I hardly drew breath until I'd finished. 'Okay, so now you know everything.'

'Why didn't you tell me all this before?' she demanded. Then, in a hurt voice, she added, 'I suppose you thought I'd go round blabbing to everyone.'

'Milly, how could you even suggest such a thing?'

'I thought we were best friends,' she continued, 'and best friends always share their secrets with each other... don't they?'

'You're right Milly, but when I started, the only thing I had to go on was Dad's papers and a hunch. I thought if I told anyone else, they'd think I was going bonkers.'

'As if I'd think that of you,' said Milly, 'you're one of the most sensible people I know.'

Milly, who'd calmed down by now, continued excitedly, 'Can I see what you've discovered?'

'I showed her the letter then explained how I'd spent the morning studying it, concluding most of it was just sound financial advice.'

'Most of it?' quizzed Milly.

Pointing to the last paragraph, I said, 'All except here where it says, "Fund 'A' seems open, when realigned, to unlock the prospect of a lucrative yield. Therefore, I strongly recommend you seriously consider Fund 'A' as part of your investment".' That's when my head almost exploded, and I decided to call it a day.

'Hmm,' said Milly, as she repeated the sentence over and over again, hoping for a light bulb moment.

Out of the corner of my eye, I saw Mr Crossword Man jotting something down in the margins of his newspaper. I felt certain he'd been listening. I watched as he puzzled over the words until a satisfied smile crossed his face and he exclaimed, 'Of course!' Then, leaning towards me, he whispered, 'Excuse me for eavesdropping, but I'm a bit of a crossword buff. I especially enjoy solving cryptic clues.'

'Cryptic clues?' I asked.

'Yes,' he said, 'whoever wrote this has hidden a message in one of the sentences. It appears to be an anagram of "A seems open". If I could, I'd sit and solve it with you, but I'm in a bit of a rush and haven't got the time. But if you play around with the words, you'll soon find the answer. If you're still really struggling, there's plenty of anagram generators available on the internet. As for "to unlock the prospect of lucrative yields", I can only assume, once you've solved the anagram, the answer will enable you to unlock something.'

Folding his paper, he stood up and said, 'Sorry, girls, but for the moment, that's the best I can do. Hope I've been of some assistance. Have a nice day.'

When he'd finally gone, Milly asked, 'What the hell was he babbling on about?'

'I think he's just given us the key to unlocking Dad's laptop!' I said, excitedly.

Noticing I hadn't touched my packed lunch, she asked, 'Do you want some of my chips?'

With the smell of salt and vinegar playing havoc with my gastric juices, I said, 'Don't mind if I do!' Then, much to Milly's dismay, I grabbed a handful of chips and greedily stuffed them into my mouth. If you'd like to know what happened to the fish paste sandwiches, you're going to have to ask the pigeons!

CHAPTER FIFTEEN

'Ted... come quick. You'll never guess who's on telly.'

'I'm busy, can't it wait?' shouted Ted, angrily, 'I've got to wear asbestos gloves, this Ferrari's so hot. We need to have it off the premises and out of the country by tomorrow before the police come sniffing round.'

'It won't take long, I promise. Hurry up or you'll miss it.'

Ted dropped what he was doing and joined Fergie in their makeshift office. Growling angrily, he said, 'This'd better be worth it.'

Pointing to the telly, Fergie said, 'Look who it is.'

Ted pushed his face up close to the screen, squinted, then said, 'That's the Brown kid, isn't it. What's she doing on the telly?'

'Some rubbish about a sissy playing in a girls' football team.'

When the interview was over, Ted said, 'She's a clever little bitch, that one. She doesn't get her brains from her mother, that's for certain. I reckon if that dirty, double-crossing rat of a father was going to tell anybody where he'd stashed our money, it'd be her. If you ask me, I still think the information's stored on his laptop. One of my contacts in the police told me they'd tried everything to try and unlock it, but in the end, they were forced to give it up as a bad job.'

'If what you say is true,' said an unusually lucid Fergie, 'then we need to get our hands on that laptop!'

'Have you been eating a lot of fish lately?' asked Ted.

'I had a chippy supper last Friday if that's what you mean. Why are you asking?'

'Because you've just presented me with the germ of a plan.'

'What's eating a fish supper got to do with it?' asked Fergie.

~~~

Feeling proud of myself, I arrived home in a buoyant mood.

'Did you manage to finish that project?' asked Mum.

'Not yet, I've still got some more writing up to do, but with the information I managed to gather, I reckon I'm nailed on for a straight A.'

'Did you enjoy your sandwiches?'

Oh oh, one of Mum's loaded questions. Think quickly. 'Yes, they were gorgeous. What kind of fish was it?'

'I haven't a Scooby, it was all written in Chinese. They were selling them off cheap at the Asian supermarket. They were still in date so it should be okay. Where did you go to eat them?'

'I decided to go into town and eat them on one of the benches, but the place was chocka, so I had to wait for a seat. When I finally found one, Milly's mum spotted me, so me and Milly sat together and ate our lunch while her mum continued shopping.'

I'd told Mum a few porkies of late, so I decided that telling her one more wasn't going to make a difference. I might as well be hung for a sheep as a lamb.

With only the flimsiest of evidence, Mum has this uncanny knack of putting two and two together then interrogating me to within an inch of my life until she finally forces me into making a full confession.

So, when she asked, 'What did Milly have for lunch?' I'd already prepared my answer.

'A jumbo hot dog!' I replied, confidently.

I know it sounds devious but if it meant mum not sussing out, I'd binned her sandwiches and ate some of Milly's chips instead, then it would be worth it.

'She probably bought it off that bloke with the hot dog stand at the back of Booze Busters.'

'I couldn't tell you where it came from. Her mum bought it for her.'

'He stands there all day selling hot dogs and hamburgers,' she continued, 'yet nobody ever sees him going to the toilet.'

'Maybe he's got a large bladder.'

'Large bladder, my foot. Some people say he has a bottle under the counter that he wees in. Others think he does it somewhere else!'

'Where else could he do it?'

'All I can say is... avoid the onions at all costs!'

'Give him a break, Mum, he's only trying to make a living.'

'Well, he's not making a living out of me! At least you know where your sandwiches came from.'

'And where they went,' I muttered.

'What did you say?'

'I said, 'That was money well spent.'

'Oh... well... that's all right then.'

Now that Mum was off my case, all that remained was for me to find the password. Doing exactly what Mr Crossword Man had told me, I searched online for an anagram generator and, true to his word, a full page of options appeared. I selected one, opened it and typed in 'A seems open'. Among the list of anagram solutions, I saw, Open Sesame. It was so blindingly obvious, I wondered why I hadn't figured it out in the first place. Especially as Dad had given me a big clue with Alibaba. I fired up dad's laptop and when it asked for the password, I entered Open Sesame and... Bingo, I was in. But where to next?

I spent the next few hours going round and round in circles. Every time I opened a file, I'd be overwhelmed with pages and pages of spreadsheets, financial data and client details. In frustration, I decided to call it a day. Maybe after a good night's sleep, I'd see things differently.

~~~

Ted parked the beamer far enough away from our house so as not to be noticed.

'Hurry up and finish your breakfast,' said Mum, 'I'm running late.'

As usual, Mum didn't have a minute to spare. I waited outside while she gathered her bits and bobs.

'You've not seen my handbag, have you?' she shouted.

'Last time I saw it, it was on the sideboard,' I countered.

'I can see it now. I'll just check if all the windows and doors are locked, then I'll be with you.'

'You've already done it!'

'Well, you can't be too careful.'

She stepped out onto the street, slammed the door behind her then unlocked the car. Taking my place in the front seat, I watched, arms folded, seatbelt buckled, as she attempted to clear a space on the back seat for her things. Once satisfied, she positioned herself behind the steering wheel. Checking her hair and makeup, then gritting her teeth and drawing a deep breath, she turned the key in the ignition.

The engine gave a high-pitched screech, then cut out. Ignoring its pitiful screams for mercy, she repeated the procedure until, reluctantly, it spluttered into life. Sensing victory, she pressed home her advantage by revving the bejesus out of it.

~~~

As they patiently waited, Ted quietly puffed on his vape while Fergie studied the Daily Sport's babe of the day.

'We've crushed better cars than that,' observed Ted. 'As soon as that heap of junk's out of sight, we'll nip round the back and have a mooch.'

'What if someone sees us?'

'Just say we're from the council.'

They waited for the last of the exhaust fumes to disappear then Ted said, 'Okay, the coast's clear, let's go.' They climbed out of the car and, not wanting to attract any unwanted attention, they casually strolled to the corner. A swift glance down the alley was all Ted needed. 'Not a soul in sight. This should be a piece of cake.'

When they reached our gate, Ted slowly lifted the latch and pushed against it. It was unbolted. They hurried to the back door then searched for an easy way in. 'I can't believe our luck,' laughed Ted, 'they've still got the old-fashioned wooden sash windows. They might just as well have left the key in the door.'

Ted pulled a pen knife from his pocket, pushed it through the gap between the sashes and eased open the window. 'Okay,' said Ted, leaning on the window ledge. 'I've done my bit, now it's your turn.' In next to no time, Fergie was through the window and unlocking the back door.

They moved swiftly through the house, grabbing anything remotely resembling a laptop. They packed them into one of

Mum's old suitcases then leaving by the front door, casually walked the short distance to Ted's car. Placing the suitcase in the boot, they sped off down the road.

'Do you think anybody saw us?' asked a nervous Fergie.

'No,' answered Ted. 'They only notice when you're either acting suspicious or running.'

'Even though we were dragging a suitcase behind us?'

'They'd probably think we were door-to-door salesmen selling encyclopaedias or something.'

'Do people actually go round selling encyclopaedias?'

'They used to,' replied, Ted, 'but that was before Google.'

'Some people think I look shifty,' mused Fergie.

Ted glanced at Fergie's three-day stubble, frayed cuffs and egg-stained tie and, finding himself lost for words, drew deeply on his vape.

Ted had a wry smile on his face as he drove along, humming a tuneless ditty, prompting Fergie to comment. 'You sound happy today, Ted.'

'It never leaves you,' said Ted, smugly. 'I might have been out of the game for a few years, but I still haven't lost my touch.'

'I've been meaning to ask you something for a long time.'

'What's that, Fergie?'

'How did you manage to cotton on to this racket?'

'After I was sent down for the third time, I thought to myself, Ted, me lad, don't you think you're getting a bit too old for this game. Isn't it time you found yourself another caper? And that's exactly what I did. And ever since then, I've never looked back.'

'But surely there's enough money to be made out of scrap metal without having to do all this dodgy stuff?'

'You're right, Fergie, there is. But where's the fun in that?'

~~~

'When exactly did you discover you'd been burgled, Mrs Brown?' asked Inspector Maitland.

'My last client was at three, so I called at Aldi before I picked up Rosie from school. We must have got back at around four o'clock. Didn't we, Rosie?'

'Yes, it was about four, Mum.'

'I know it was four because I was listening to the radio at the time and the four o'clock news had just started. That's right, isn't it, Rosie?'

'Yes, Mum.'

'I distinctly remember opening the front door and Rosie running upstairs to change, then I went back to the car to collect the shopping. That's when Rosie shouted, Have you seen my laptop, Mum? And I said, The last time I saw it, it was on your desk. That's right, isn't it, Rosie?'

'Yes, Mum.'

'So, Rosie ran upstairs to have another look. Didn't you, love?'

This time, I just nodded.

'I ran in and dropped the shopping on the couch. While Rosie was still upstairs, I thought I'd check my emails, so I went to the sideboard, opened the drawer and there it was—gone! I know it was in there this morning because I remember putting it in there before I left the house. That's when I put two and two together and realised we'd been burgled. Thinking they could still be in the house, I picked up a poker from out of the fireplace and opened the kitchen door. That's when I saw the curtains fluttering in the breeze. Not showing a morsel of fear, and taking my life in my own hands, I ran into the kitchen and slammed the window shut. Then, locking the back door, I ran back into the living room and rang 999.'

'You should have left everything as it was until the police arrived.'

'I was worried they might be outside in the yard.'

'Quite understandable, Mrs Brown,' he replied, 'but it hasn't made our job any easier.'

'Have you made a list of what's been stolen?' he continued.

'I've had a quick look round and it looks like the only things missing are our laptops.'

'Does that mean only two laptops were stolen?'

'Yes,' said Mum.

'No,' I said, 'I think they've taken Dad's as well.'

'Is that the one we returned to you?' asked the inspector.

'Yes,' I replied.

Before he could ask any more questions, there was a knock at the door. When Mum opened it, she found two people wearing Tyvek suits.

'We're from the CSI. Can we come in, please?'

Inspector Maitland, who'd followed her to the door, said, 'I've asked the CSI team to come and take a look around—if that's all right with you, Mrs Brown.'

'Yes, of course,' she replied.

I'd been dreading having to face the inspector's questions, so the timely arrival of the CSI team was a welcome distraction. Having survived endless grillings by Mum, a cross examination by Inspector Maitland ought to be a piece of cake.

While they were busy gathering evidence, the inspector returned to further his inquiries, but this time, he focused on me.

'Rosie,' he asked, 'where did you keep your dad's laptop?'

'I kept it in my room.'

'Why did you do that when you don't even know the password?'

'I thought, maybe if I fiddled about with it long enough, I might somehow come up with the password.'

'Even though you knew it had defeated our best computer technicians?'

'Yes.'

'And were you anymore successful?' he asked, suspiciously.

194

'No,' I lied.

'It seems very strange that nothing else of value was stolen. My gut feeling is that somebody's desperate to get hold of that laptop, and they're prepared to go to any lengths to find out what's in it.'

Standing up, he folded his notebook and said, 'That's all for now, Mrs Brown.'

'When will I find out what's happening?' asked Mum.

'I've just got to wait for the forensic results then I'll be able to report back to you. If it turns out to be the work of local villains, then it's just a simple a matter of rounding them up, searching their homes, and putting them under lock and key.'

'By the time you catch them, they'll have fenced the lot.'

'We know who all the local dealers in stolen goods are, Mrs Brown, and I can assure you they wouldn't touch a hooky laptop with a barge pole.'

Then he looked me squarely in the eyes and said, 'I'll ask you one more time, Rosie. Do you know your dad's password?'

'No,' I gulped.

CHAPTER SIXTEEN

'Okay, Ted, we've got the laptops, but which is the one we're looking for?'

'Come on, Fergie, get real, use your common sense. Two of them are Aldi specials and one's an Apple. I know it's had a bit of a battering, but it's an Apple all the same, and probably worth over a grand.'

'If you knew that, then why did we have to take these crap ones as well?'

'Two reasons, Fergie me boy. Firstly, if we only took the Apple, it wouldn't take the plod very long to figure out it was the only reason we broke into the house. And secondly, you never know, there could be some useful information stored on the others. Don't forget, stealing them was the easy bit, now we have to find a way to get into them. Luckily, I've got a mate who's in the computer game. I'll get him to have a look at them.'

~~~

I'm rarely fazed, but the burglary had really shaken me. It wasn't just the loss of my laptop, which only had the speed of a sloth and the memory of a goldfish. What had really upset me was the thought of somebody entering my room and rummaging through my personal belongings.

I was convinced Ted and Fergie were behind it and wondered whether it was time I told Mum. The trouble was, if I did tell her, she'd only go into a blind panic, report it to the police, then one way or another, Ted would somehow get wind of it, and I'd lose my advantage. No, this was something I needed to do on my own—and with Milly, of course!

Mum's never been very computer savvy. She only ever used hers for emails and Googling while I, on the other hand, have always been ultra careful where online security is concerned. Every time I'd used my computer, Dad would come along to see what I was up to, then lecture me on cyber security, so I always make sure I'm up to date with my antivirus and malware protection. Just to be on the safe side, I'd registered both mine and Mum's laptops with a tracking service just in case they were ever lost or stolen.

While the inspector was questioning Mum, he'd asked her if she knew whether they could be traced, but she just shrugged and said, 'I haven't a clue about all that computer stuff. I always left that sort of thing to John.' In reality, I was the one he should have been asking, but for some reason he never got round to it—and I certainly wasn't going to volunteer the information.

Having done all the donkey work, there was no way I was going to allow Inspector Maitland to take the glory. If it was Ted and Fergie who were behind the robbery, then I was determined to find out for myself. Unbeknown to both Ted and the police, I had an ace up my sleeve. And with a bit of luck, and the help of Milly's iPad, we ought be able to locate the laptops and catch the robbers at the same time—at least that was my plan.

'Hi, Mrs Hampson; its Rosie, is Milly in?'

'She's in her room. Or at least, that's where she was the last time I saw her. Hold on a minute while I give her a shout.'

I could hear the TV in the background and the indistinct sound of Mrs Hampson calling, 'Milly, are you up there?'

'Yes,' echoed a familiar voice.

'It's your friend, Rosie, she's on the phone.'

I heard the pounding of feet on stairs, swiftly followed by the panting voice of Milly. 'Hi, Rosie. I was upstairs playing on my computer, what do you want?'

'I've got a problem and I need your help.'

'Always ready to oblige,' chirped Milly.

'Can you come round to ours and bring your iPad with you? You'll need some warm clothes and sturdy shoes just in case we have to do some walking.'

'What's it all about?' asked a puzzled Milly.

Cupping my hand over the mouthpiece, I whispered, 'Can't talk over the phone, I'll tell you more when you get here.'

'It all sounds very hush-hush,' she replied, 'can't wait to find out what it's all about. I'll be over as soon as.'

Before she could put the phone down, I yelled, 'Don't forget your iPad! It's very important you bring it with you.'

When she arrived, I grabbed a couple of cans of Coke from the fridge and we went up to my room.

'Okay, Rosie. Time to spill the beans.'

I told her about the burglary and how the only things taken were our laptops. 'I want to use your iPad to try and locate their whereabouts.'

'Is there something you're not telling me?' asked an increasingly suspicious Milly.

She sat quietly as I told my story. When I'd finished, she said, 'Does your mum know any of this?'

'No, I didn't want to worry her; you're the only other person who knows.'

'Why didn't you tell me earlier?' she asked, 'after all, we are supposed to be friends.'

'We are friends, that's why I'm telling you now.'

'It looks as if you only decided to tell me now so you could use my iPad.'

'That's not true, Milly. I've been dying to tell you for ages. I was only waiting for the right time—and now is the right time.'

'So, what makes you think Ted and Fergie are at the bottom of this?'

'I don't. The only way I'm going to find out is by trying to locate the laptops.'

'I believe you, thousands wouldn't. There's no time like the present, so let's get going!'

I sat on the bed next to Milly and waited while she logged into her iPad. She typed the website into the search engine, then entered the login details. When she clicked, Find My Device, Mum's laptop appeared.

'It looks like they've managed to open Mum's laptop,' I said, 'she was never very good at choosing secure passwords! It's showing the location to be somewhere down Blackstone Lane.'

'Isn't that where the gypsy camp is?' exclaimed Milly.

'Difficult to tell on this map. I think we need to be a bit closer to know for certain.'

The dropdown menu offered three options: Sound alarm, Send message and Lock device.

'Shouldn't we lock it so they can't use it?' asked Milly.

'No,' I said, 'if we do, they'd know we're on to them. And anyway, there's not very much on Mum's laptop.'

'It looks like it was the gypsies all along,' said Milly, smugly, 'and who do we know that lives there?'

'Surely you don't think the twins had anything to do with it!' I exclaimed.

'If the shoe fits ...!'

'How can you even think such a thing?' I said, 'they're our best friends.'

'Tell you what,' suggested Milly, 'why don't we kill two birds with one stone and pay them a visit? Then while we're there we can have a snoop round the camp.'

'Good idea,' I replied, 'they'll be made up to see us. I'll grab my coat and if we're quick we might be in time to catch the next bus.'

'I'd best leave Mum a note,' I said, 'just so she knows where we've gone.'

We arrived at the terminus with seconds to spare and breathlessly jumped onto the bus. 'Two halves to Blackstone Lane, please?' I gasped, 'and could you give us a shout when we're almost there?'

'Certainly, ladies. Wouldn't want you to miss your stop, would I?'

'Thank you, driver.'

'You're welcome.'

Twenty minutes later, we were walking down Blackstone Lane. By the time we'd reached the farmhouse, Milly was already lagging behind.

'Come on, Milly, best foot forward,' I shouted.

'Can we stop for a few minutes?' pleaded Milly, 'my best foot and its mate are killing me.'

'Okay,' I said, 'but we can't hang about for long; we don't want to be walking back in the dark.'

'It's these bloody shoes,' she complained, 'if I'd have known we'd be walking this far I wouldn't have worn them.'

'Didn't I tell you to wear sturdy shoes?'

'These are the sturdiest I've got.'

'Oh well, there's not much we can do about it now.'

We continued walking until, once again, Milly stopped, gasping, 'How long before we get there?'

'Not long now,' I said, 'once we reach the corrugated fence, it's a hop, a skip and a jump to the camp.'

'It's hard enough walking, never mind all this hopping, skipping and jumping,' she grumbled.

When we reached the lane entrance, I pointed and said, 'It's only a short way from here.'

'Thank God for that,' she groaned.

As the camp came into view, I said, 'Before we enter the lion's den, why don't we check the tracker again? It might give us a better idea where they've hidden the laptops.'

Milly sat on a fence, took out her iPad and turned on the tracking app. This time the map was more precise. It showed, in vivid detail, the camp and the surrounding area. To our surprise, the indicator wasn't pointing into the gypsy camp as we'd first thought. Instead, it indicated the laptops were somewhere behind the corrugated fence.

'They must have stashed them in there,' I said, pointing to the fence. 'Let's go back and see if we can find a way in; that's if your feet are up to it.'

'As luck would have it, I've brought a spare pair of socks with me,' replied Milly, 'give me a minute while I put them on.'

I could see Milly was starting to regret coming so, giving her hand a reassuring squeeze, I put my arm round her shoulder, and we walked the lane together.

Upon reaching Blackstone Road, we turned left and walked a little further until we arrived at a gravel drive with a sign, which read:

Blackstone Vehicle Recycling Centre

Top prices paid for MOT failures and insurance write offs

Proprietor: Mr E. Murphy

The large corrugated double gates were secured with a heavy padlock and chain. Danger Keep Out had been daubed in runny red paint across the gate's corrugations. Peering through the gap, I could see vehicles of every shape and size haphazardly stacked in maze-like rows.

'If we could find something to poke through this gap,' I explained, 'we ought to be able to prise them open. And with a bit of luck, we should be able to squeeze through.'

'You might,' said Milly, 'I'd probably get stuck halfway.'

'Don't be silly,' I replied, 'you'll easily fit through.'

'You go first,' suggested Milly, 'then once you're inside you might be able to open the gates a bit further. One question—what are we going to use to open it?'

'I thought you might ask that,' I replied. 'When we were walking towards the gypsy camp, I noticed a scaffolding pole sticking out of a ditch. Let's go back and get it.'

Milly looked at her watch, then at the darkening skies, and replied, 'Do you think we've got enough time?'

Having come this far, I was reluctant to turn back, so I said, 'If we act quickly, we'll be in, find the laptops, then out again before they even realise what's happened.'

We hurried to where I'd seen the pole. This time Milly was keeping pace. 'Looks like those socks have done the trick,' I said. Then, pointing to the ditch, I exclaimed, 'Here it is!'

'I've got a bad feeling about this,' said Milly as we climbed down the bank. 'I just want to get it over and done with and get back home.'

'Stop being such a wet lettuce and grab hold of it with me. Once it's out we can carry it back to the gate.'

The pole was wedged deep into the bed of the ditch. 'We're never going to get it out,' moaned Milly.

'Just keep waggling it backwards and forwards and it'll soon be out.'

With a slurp, a gurgle and an acrid stench of foul air, reluctantly, the ditch released its grip, and the pole came free. Still clutching the pole, we ended up in a heap on the bank.

'Who's going to hold the slimy end?' asked Milly.

'I'd normally say we toss a coin for it but as I asked you to come along, I suppose it'll have to be me.'

'There's an old vest or something lying over there,' pointed Milly, 'why don't you wrap it round the end of the pole, so you don't get covered in gunge?'

'Good idea, Milly.'

So, with several rests along the way, mostly at Milly's request, we finally made it to the scrap yard.

Rubbing her arms, Milly gasped, 'Hell's bells, Rosie, this thing weighs a flippin' ton.'

'That's because it's a scaffold pole, they're supposed to be heavy.'

I peeled the vest off the end of the pole then, letting out a scream of disgust, I flung the repulsive garment into a nearby bush.

'What is it, Rosie?'

'You know that old vest we found?'

'Yes.'

'Well, it turns out it wasn't a vest.'

'What was it then?'

'A pair of soiled underpants!'

'Urgh! You've not got any on your hands, have you?'

I gave them a quick sniff, then said, 'It doesn't smell like it. Anyway, forget about my hands, we need to concentrate on finding what we came here for.'

We pushed the pole through the gap and wedged it into the ground on the far side of the gate. Then we started pushing.

'Is it moving?' gasped Milly.

'I think so, but it's still not wide enough for us to get through. I think we're doing this all wrong. What we should really be doing is facing the other way and pulling instead of pushing.'

Like two galley slaves waiting for the drummer to start, we took a firm grip of the pole. 'Ready when you are,' I whispered ... then I started pulling.

The gate creaked, groaned, moaned, and grumbled, but it stubbornly refused to move. Once again, we dug in our heels, then I shouted, 'Heave!'

The gate emitted an ear-splitting screech, but it still didn't yield. 'It's no good' cried Milly, 'it's not going to go.'

'We can't give up now,' I said, 'let's give it one last go and if we still can't force it open, we'll go back home.'

'Okay,' said Milly, 'one last go!'

Knowing this was the final throw of the dice, we dug in our heels, and braced ourselves for a herculean effort. 'On the count of three ... one, two, three ...Heave!'

Straining every muscle and sinew, we pulled as if our lives depended on it. There was an almighty crack, then the pole flew out of our hands, sending us sprawling onto the ground.

I stood up and dusted myself down. Then, looking at my bedraggled friend sitting beside me, I asked, 'Are you all right?'

'I'll live,' she groaned.

I helped her to her feet then inspected the damage, 'We've done it!' I shouted, pointing to a gaping chasm in the gate. 'Come on, Milly, no time to waste, let's go and have a quick look round.'

Vehicles of every shape and size were stacked haphazardly in chaotic rows, all waiting to be either dismantled or crushed. Ahead, a fork truck and grabber were silently parked next to the crusher, waiting to feed the ravenous mechanical beast.

With Milly close behind, I strode straight past their Portakabin and into the yard. 'Shouldn't we be looking in there?' asked Milly, pointing to the Portakabin.

'I can't see them keeping anything of value in that place,' I replied.

'But the sign on the door says it's the office!'

'It says Coca-Cola on the side of buses, but it doesn't mean they sell it,' I said. 'Before we do anything hasty, first we need to check out the rest of the yard.'

'Where do we start?' asked Milly, gazing into the labyrinthine scrapyard. 'The whole place is like a rabbit warren.'

'Look down there,' I said, pointing to a recently surfaced road, 'there must be something down there. Why else would they have had it tarmacked? Let's walk down and see where it leads.'

We passed a multitude of precariously stacked vehicles until a smart two-storey, red-bricked building came into view.

'Look at this!' I exclaimed. 'Why on earth would they put a building like that at the back end of a scrapyard? Surely, it'd make more sense to build it closer to the entrance instead of using a tatty Portakabin as the office. They've obviously put it down here for a reason. Come on, Milly, let's go take a closer look.'

'Is it really worth it?' Milly asked. 'They've got shutters on every door and window.'

'It probably isn't worth it,' I replied, 'but as we're already here, it'd be stupid not to have a quick look round—you never know what we might find.'

'Okay,' Milly said, anxiously, 'but let's make it quick.'

As we approached, Milly whispered, 'It's very quiet!'

'Too quiet if you ask me.'

'It's more like a graveyard than a scrapyard,' continued Milly.

'When you think about it,' I mused, 'in some ways you could describe it as a graveyard... a car's graveyard!'

When we reached the building, I stood back and quietly gave it the once over. Then I said, 'It looks like some kind of workshop, but for the life of me, I still can't understand why they'd want to put it down here.'

'One thing's for certain,' said Milly, 'they don't want anybody to know what they're up to.'

'Maybe if we look round, you never know, they might have hidden a key somewhere.'

'Get real, Rosie,' said Milly, 'who in their right mind would go to the trouble of locking every window and door then leave the key under a doormat?'

'I suppose when you put it like that... but before we leave, why don't we look round the back? They could have left a window open or something.'

'You can if you like,' replied Milly, 'I'll just wait here till you get back.'

When I returned, Milly said, 'Well? Did you find anything?'

'Nothing,' I conceded, 'even if they had left the toilet window open, you'd need to be the man of steel to bend those bars!'

In desperation, I looked up to the roof to see if there might be another way in, but I was disappointed to find the gutters and downspouts were wrapped in barbed wire with signs warning intruders of the dangers.

Conceding defeat, I shrugged my shoulders and said, 'Some you win, some you lose—come on, Milly, it's time we went home.'

Milly gave a loud squeal and said, 'Wait a minute, I've just had an idea. What if we were to activate the laptop alarms? With a bit of luck, we'd be able to hear them out here, then once we were certain they're in there, we could go back and report it to the police.'

'Good thinking, Milly.' Then the doubts crept in. 'There's just one slight flaw.'

'What's that?' asked Milly.

'If I went to the police, I'd be in trouble for not telling them about the tracker, not to mention breaking and entering, criminal damage, trespassing, and whatever else they chose to throw at me. I could end up with a record as long as your arm—or worse... go to jail!'

'They don't send twelve-year-old girls to jail,' snorted Milly, 'and anyway, knowing you, you'd probably manage to talk your way out of it. So, let's not worry about it for now. Once we're safely back home, we can figure out what to do next.'

Milly logged into the tracker and from the options, she chose, 'Sound Alarm On'.

'Are you ready?' she asked.

I nodded affirmatively.

She clicked on the link then waited for what seemed like an eternity, 'Are you sure you chose the right option?' I asked.

Her eyes widened and her nostrils flared. 'Of course, I did. What do you think I am, some kind of numpty?' A distant wail began to issue from deep inside the building. Milly gave me a satisfied smirk.

Not to be outdone, I said, 'It could be an alarm clock or something.'

'It's not an alarm clock,' she snapped, 'they're much louder than that.'

'You could be right,' I said, sheepishly.

'I am right,' she declared.

'So, if we discount the possibility of it being an alarm clock, it can only be one thing... the laptop.'

'To be absolutely certain,' said Milly, 'I'll turn it off then turn it back on again.'

Milly went onto the tracker and clicked 'Sound Alarm Off'. Within seconds, the alarm fell silent. 'I told you,' smirked Milly.

'Okay, clever clogs, let's see what happens when you switch it on again,' I stubbornly replied.

She opened the app and clicked 'Sound Alarm On'. We didn't have to wait very long before we heard the echoey sound of Weeoo, Weeoo, Weeoo...

'There you are,' cried Milly, 'I was right all along. The laptops are definitely in there.'

'Quick,' I shouted, 'switch it off before somebody hears it and comes to investigate.'

Milly muted the alarm and said, 'We've done what we came for, now let's get out of here, there should be a bus along shortly.'

Not wanting to give up quite so easily, I said, 'Can't we just have one more look before we go? Another five more minutes isn't going to make any difference.'

'Only if you promise not to be any longer than five minutes,' demanded Milly.

With my arms behind my back and my fingers firmly crossed, I said, 'Promise!'

Just then we saw headlights approaching, 'Someone's coming,' exclaimed Milly.

'No panic,' I replied, 'they're probably going to the gypsy camp.'

We watched and waited, hoping the lights would disappear down the lane to the camp, but to our horror they veered towards the yard.

'Hell's fire, they're coming here!' I exclaimed.

'I told you we should have left when we had the chance,' panicked Milly.

'It's too late now, we'll just have to find somewhere to hide until they go away.'

By this time, the approaching car was crunching down the drive. Grabbing Milly's hand, we ran for cover. 'You don't think they know we're here, do you?' asked Milly.

'I doubt it, but it's too early to say,' I panted, 'as soon as they see the damaged gates, they're bound to know they've had visitors.'

From outside there came a crunch of feet on gravel, followed by the rattling of chains. Then a voice rang out, 'Ted!'

'What's up now?' roared an irate Ted.

'Come over here and have a look at this.'

'For God's sake, Fergie, I haven't got time to waste gawping at a pair of gates. Just open the bloody things so we can get the cars ready for when the transporter arrives.'

'You really do need to come over here,' insisted Fergie, 'it won't take a minute.'

'Okay,' sighed Ted, 'but it'd better be worth it.'

Ensconced behind a Lada Riva, we held our breath and listened to Ted reluctantly trudging to the gates. 'What is it you want me to see?' he growled.

'Just look at this,' said Fergie, pointing to the scaffold pole, 'somebody's been trying to break into the compound again.'

'You're right, Fergie. Luckily, it looks like the gates were too strong for them.'

'They've still managed to snap the drop bolt though,' observed Fergie, 'and now there's a wide gap in the gates.'

'It should be secure enough for tonight,' said Ted. 'I'll get someone to come round first thing in the morning to fix it.'

'It'll be those gypsy kids again,' concluded Fergie, 'they're always up to mischief.'

As soon as Fergie opened the gates, the headlights carved a swath through the yard. By this time, we'd managed to conceal ourselves in an old Transit van. Curious to find out what was happening, I peered out. I was dazzled by the glare of the headlights but felt certain I'd heard them calling each other Fergie and Ted.

Once inside, Fergie shut the gates and joined Ted in the car. 'The last thing we want is prying eyes. Especially tonight,' said Ted.

'I wonder what's so special about tonight.' I whispered.

'Whatever it is,' replied Milly, 'I hope we're miles away when it happens.'

'It looks like we're going to have to hang about a little longer until it's safe to go,' I continued, 'so we might as well sit back and make ourselves comfortable.'

'In here!' exclaimed Milly, 'it stinks of cat pee and sick.'

'I know, but what can we do?'

'I can't stay in here for long,' protested Milly, 'I'm bursting for a wee.'

'Tell you what,' I said, 'while they're busy, we'll see if we can find a better place to hide. And while we're at it, find some toilets.'

Ted parked opposite the workshop and, with the headlights on, set about opening up. While they were otherwise engaged, I decided to explore further. Just beyond the crusher, I spied a small breeze block outhouse. The ridges of its asbestos roof had long since disappeared under lush layers of cushion moss as if attempting to merge with the green painted door.

'I think I might just have found your toilets, Milly. So, no time like the present—let's make a dash for it.'

Reaching the crusher without any mishaps, I pointed to the toilet and said, 'While you're having your wee, I'll go and take a closer look. Won't be long!'

Before she had time to protest, I was sprinting towards the workshop, ducking and diving over, under, over, and in between the steel and glass mountains of wrecked and rusting cars. When I reached the closest stack to the workshop, I looked back and saw Milly frantically beckoning me back. But I was on a mission, and nothing was going to deter me. Pretending not to understand her signals, I returned her waves then knelt down to watch. By this time, they'd opened the roller doors and were standing with their backs to us, admiring the shiny new sports cars in the workshop.

I wonder what their game is.

Too far away to hear what was being said, I looked round for somewhere closer. The nearest place was a mesh cage attached to the wall by the roller doors. It was a storage compound for gas cylinders and welding equipment. A sign read, Flammable Materials, No Smoking. With their backs turned, I decided to break cover and make a dash for the compound.

It was now or never. So, springing to my feet, I sprinted towards the cage. With one eye on the crooks and the other on my destination, I'd failed to notice there was loose gravel and debris littering the road. When the inevitable finally happened, I went flying, headfirst through the air. Thanks to my judo training, I instinctively threw out my hands and went into a well-rehearsed dive roll then returned to my feet. But my triumph was short lived. Unable to check my momentum in time, I continued to hurtle uncontrollably towards my objective. Bracing myself, I smashed into the cage and fell in a crumpled heap to the ground. I barely had time to catch my breath before Ted was shouting, 'Did you hear something, Fergie?'

'I thought I heard a clanging noise,' he replied, 'but then again, I'm always hearing noises. It's usually those gypsy kids lobbing stones over the fence. I'm sure they only do it to annoy me.'

'Go and have a quick look round,' said Ted, 'the last thing we want is a load of kids hanging round the place. Especially tonight.'

It was now getting dark, and the damp evening air was sending shivers down my spine. I sat and waited to see what they'd do next. With his high vis jacket, hard hat and flashlight, Fergie strode purposely out of the garage. Fully focused on the task at hand, he didn't even give me a sideways glance as he disappeared up the nearest aisle. Every now and again, I'd hear his footsteps then the occasional clatter of metal and fleeting glimpses of flashlight as he scoured the yard. The longer he was out, the greater the chance he had of finding Milly. I spent a nervous ten minutes quietly watching and listening, fully expecting to hear him shout, 'I've caught one!' And I wondered what I'd do if he did. My fears were allayed when he finally emerged empty handed from the labyrinth. Keeping my head down, I watched as he slowly passed my hiding place. Just when I thought it was safe, he suddenly turned and shone the lamp directly into the gas store, casting ghostly shadows on the wall behind. Breaking into a cold sweat, I desperately looked for a means of escape. But instead of him saying, 'I can see you, come out or else...', he started whistling a nondescript tune as he switched off the lamp and returned to the workshop.

'Did you see anything?' asked Ted.

'Not a dicky bird,' he jauntily replied.

'Are you certain there's nobody about?' demanded Ted.

'As certain as I'll ever be.'

'Then that's good enough for me,' he sighed. 'Okay, Fergie, it's time to get cracking. They'll be here soon.'

I was hurting all over. So, in an effort to prioritise my injuries, I made a feeble attempt at self-triaging. Apart from a few superficial bruises, my worst injuries were torn Jeans, a few cuts and grazes, and my dented pride. So, settling down in the corner, I took out a pack of tissues and, using Mum's patented spit-and-wash method, I tended to my wounds.

Mum'll go ballistic when she sees the state of me, I thought.

It had all gone quiet in the workshop, and I was beginning to feel better. From what I'd heard, tonight was going to be a nice little earner, but I still didn't know what they were up to.

I'd promised Milly we'd leave as soon as we got the chance but finding Ted, Fergie and the laptops together in one place was more than just coincidence. And too good an opportunity to miss.

Dusting myself down, I crept to the door and listened. 'That's the Maserati sorted,' said Ted, 'all that's left is the paperwork then they're ready to be shipped out to their new owners.'

'When do you think we'll get the money?' asked Fergie.

'It'll probably take a couple of weeks. They'll only transfer the cash once they're completely satisfied with their new acquisitions.'

'How do we know they can be trusted?' continued Fergie.

'Once these people shake on a deal, they never go back on their word.'

'My old man once said to me, "Victor, for what it's worth, here's a piece of advice: never trust anybody, especially where money's concerned." And you know what, Ted? It's never let me down.'

'Let me give you a piece of advice of my own—these guys mean business, so if you ever think of crossing them, DON'T, or you won't be around long enough to regret it.'

Fergie jumped into the driving seat of the Maserati, gripped the steering wheel, and like a stupid kid, started making broom, broom noises. 'Bet I'd be a right babe magnet driving round in one of these.'

'OUT OF THAT CAR... NOW!' ordered Ted. 'How many times do I have to tell you? Always wear clean coveralls, shoes and gloves when you sit inside one of these cars. I've not spent a fortune having them valeted just so a toe rag like you can mess them up again.'

Reluctantly, Fergie climbed out then asked, 'When's the transporter due?'

'Shouldn't be long now,' replied Ted, checking his watch. 'I'll not be happy till it's fully loaded and on its way to the docks.'

In the distance, I heard the rumbling approach of a heavy vehicle. 'Speak of the devil,' said Ted, 'that sounds like them now. Let's go.'

Suddenly, Fergie cried out, 'Hang on a minute, Ted. What's this laptop doing out on the bench?'

'That must have been me,' groaned Ted. 'Is it any wonder I forgot about it, having spent most of the afternoon trawling through the thing? In the end I felt one of my migraines coming on and went upstairs to sit in a darkened room with a packet of paracetamols and a glass of whisky, hoping it would go away.'

'Did you find anything interesting?'

'Interesting? You've got to be bloody joking! If what's on that woman's laptop is anything to go by, she's got to be one of the most boring women in Warringsley. Is it any wonder I've got a headache?'

'If it's full of rubbish,' asked Fergie, 'then why don't you just pitch it in the skip?'

'There's a couple of files I've still not looked at yet, but once I've checked them out I'll gladly lash it into the crusher. Give me a minute while I take it upstairs then I'll meet you at the gates.'

CHAPTER SEVENTEEN

Like an injured animal, I crawled into a corner to tend to my wounds. Meanwhile, outside the gates, the irate driver was angrily revving his engine and blaring the horn. It wouldn't be long before Ted and Fergie were forced to exit the building and head towards the gates.

Digging deep into my inner reserves, I climbed to my feet and waited for the opportunity to present itself. Once they'd vacated the building, the countdown would begin, then I'd be in a race against time to locate the laptops and make my escape.

Fergie was the first to show his face.

'Hurry up and get those bloody gates open,' shouted Ted, 'before we know where we are, the whole world and his dog will be round here wondering what the hell's going on.'

'Okay, Ted.'

'And while you're at it, ask them to turn down the racket. Tell them I'll be with them in a tick.'

I watched Fergie disappear into the gloom then waited for Ted to appear. One tick became two, then three, and still no sign of

Ted. With time slipping away, it was now or never. So I left the compound and, pressing my back against the wall, eased my way towards the entrance. Above the hubbub, the high-pitched screech of steel on gravel rent the air, indicating that Fergie was struggling to open the damaged gates. But where was Ted?

With the racket having subsided, I paused at the entrance and strained my ears, listening for signs of movement. Apart from the low rumble of the juggernaut's engine, it was as quiet as the grave. Confident Ted must be otherwise engaged, I cautiously entered the building and looked round. To my surprise, lined up, side by side, were four top-of-the-range sports cars. There was a maserati, a Porsche and two gleaming Ferrari's. The remainder of the garage was taken up by work benches and state-of-the-art automotive equipment.

During those idyllic days before my life was forever altered, Dad had been a supercar fanatic. I can hardly remember a time when there wasn't a car magazine or glossy brochure lying around the house.

Whenever he took me out for a Sunday drive, we'd invariably end up at a sports car showroom. Wearing his trademark fedora, shades, double-breasted blazer, open necked shirt, and cravat, he'd exuded an aristocratic air. Once inside, he'd move from car to car saying things like, 'Which one do you prefer, Jocasta? The McLaren or the Aston Martin?'

'But Dad, my name's not Jocasta!'

'Shush... someone might hear you. Just keep quiet and let me do the talking.'

With the eager salesman hanging on his every word, he'd examine each make and model, asking about performance statistics, body styles, colour options, trim levels, and countless other details. Then he'd finish by saying, 'How long does it take to get from 0 to 60?'

Just before he disappeared, I asked Dad why he spent so much time in sports car showrooms when he knew he could never afford one. He gave me a mischievous wink, tapped the side of his nose, then said, 'If all goes to plan, we'll soon be sipping Champagne for breakfast and living in the lap of luxury.'

My sole objective had been to find the laptops, get back to Milly, then disappear into thin air. But as soon as I saw these gorgeous cars, my eyes glazed over as I recalled the good times when, as Jocasta, I'd stand in the showroom holding Dad's hand while he fired question after question at the salesman. Making a beeline for the Lamborghini, I cupped my hands over the windscreen and peered inside. Then, gently caressing the paintwork, I circled the car until I arrived at the driver's door.

Should I or shouldn't I? Why not? A few more minutes isn't going to make any difference.

Knowing my obsessive curiosity could be my downfall, I found myself unable to resist the temptation. So, throwing caution to the wind, I grabbed the handle and gave it a tug. To my surprise, the door slid open to reveal its luxurious interior. With one hand on the driver's seat and the other on the steering wheel, I leaned inside and was rewarded by the heady aroma of leather upholstery and polished oak. Then my thoughts slowly drifted to happier times.

Can I sit behind the wheel, Dad?

Can she?

Certainly, sir!

As I climbed into the driver's seat, a tingle of anticipation ran through my body. Placing one hand on the gear stick and the other on the steering wheel, I inserted the non-existent key into the ignition and, with a satisfied smile, I imagined the V10 engine roaring into life.

Doors slammed, keys jangled and the sound of footsteps reverberated throughout the building. *Oh hell, it's Ted!*

With no obvious means of escape, I slid into the footwell and buried my head under the dashboard. Then I held my breath as Ted approached, not realising the vapour from my breath could be my downfall. When Ted saw rivulets of condensation trickling down the inner surface of the windscreen, he almost blew a gasket.

'That blithering idiot's been sitting in the Mazzer again,' he roared. 'When I get hold of him he'll wish he'd never been born.'

He vented his frustration on a nearby stack of tyres, then stormed out of the building.

Phew, that was close!

Checking my watch, I realised just how much time I'd wasted. So, starting in the workshop, I commenced my search. As this was a backstreet scrapyard, I'd expected to find dirty overalls, oily rags and vehicle parts untidily spread across the benches and floors. But instead, the whole room was unnaturally clean; so clean you could have eaten your dinner off the floor. Tools and equipment hung on neatly labelled racks. Posters on the whitewashed walls declared: A Tidy Place is A Safe Place and Keep This Area Clean And Tidy. Lying on the bench I saw what I thought was a laptop, but it turned out to be part of their diagnostic equipment.

At the back of the building, a steel stairway led up to a small observation platform overlooking the workshop, adjacent to which a closed door provided access to the first-floor offices. Mounting the stairs, two steps at a time, I was soon standing on the landing, preparing myself for the next obstacle—the office door. To my surprise, a bunch of keys had been left hanging in the lock.

I turned the key and, pushing open the door, revealed a dimly lit corridor. To my right, the magnolia wall was lined with framed photographs of famous racing drivers and their classic cars. To my left, were two office doors. At the far end, there was a door with a polished brass name plate, which proudly declared: General Manager.

Instantly dismissing the other doors, I headed straight for the manager's office, deducing that if the laptops were going to be anywhere, they had to be in here.

The urgency of the situation was brought into sharp focus when a robotic voice came echoing down the yard, announcing, 'Caution, this vehicle is reversing, beep — beep — beep... Caution, this vehicle is reversing...'

With only the dim glow of the emergency lighting to guide me, I tried the handle, only to find it locked. I hurried back to the first door and retrieved the keys. With only four to choose from, it was Murphy's Law that it happened to be the last one I tried.

I opened the door and ahead of me lay a desk, behind which was a stationery cupboard, two filing cabinets, a fridge-freezer, a safe, a coffee machine, and a soft drinks dispenser. On the wall above, there was a year planner, a noticeboard and a calendar. The sight of the drinks dispenser reminded me just how thirsty I'd become so, making a beeline for the machine, I selected the only flavour available—Limeade. It hadn't had enough time to touch the sides before I was thirstily downing another tumblerful. To my right, an observation window provided both a bird's-eye view of the workshop and just enough light to illuminate the room.

Below the window stood a printer and a photocopier. Squeezed between the shredder and the waste recycling bin, was ream upon ream of printing paper.

On the wall opposite, looking strangely out of place amid the orderly shelves, was a locked and shuttered window.

Positioned between the door I'd just entered, and another door leading to the adjoining offices, was a wall-mounted television.

In the meantime, the driver was growing increasingly impatient and resumed honking his horn.

'Quick, Fergie,' urged Ted, 'let's get these bleeding gates open before everybody for miles around rolls up to see what all the commotion's about.'

'They were hard enough to open before, but since those gypsy kids broke the hinges, they're even worse.'

Fergie, looking pleadingly at Ted, said, 'It'd open a lot easier if you gave me a hand.'

'What... with my bad back... you must be joking!'

He was about to resume when Ted grabbed his arm. 'Wait a minute, Fergie, we need to make sure they're kosher before we let them in.'

'Thank heavens for that, me back's killin' me.'

Wearing polished brown leather brogues, Ted winced as he gingerly crossed the rough gravel track to where the driver was waiting. Waving his arms in the air, Ted shouted, 'Turn off your engine and stop honking that horn, they'll be able to hear you in Warringsley!'

Ted hobbled back to Fergie and whispered, 'I'm not sure I like the look of these two, they're not our regular drivers. Don't open the gates till I find out who they are and where they're from.'

'Why don't I go instead?' suggested Fergie, 'you're going to ruin your feet walking on that hardcore.'

'No! you wait here and I'll check them out,' insisted Ted, 'I've got a nose for that sort of thing.'

Fergie took a long hard look at Ted's bulbous nose then replied, 'So I see!'

Carefully choosing his route, Ted walked back to the driver and indicated for him to switch off his engine. Complying, he opened his window, leaned out and asked, 'What's wrong, boss?'

'Can you show me some ID?'

'No problem, boss.'

He produced a clipboard and handed it to Ted. Ted thumbed through the documents then, still not satisfied, asked, 'Which one are you? Desislav or Aleksi?'

'I am Desislav, but everyone call me Desi.' Then, pointing to his co-driver, he said, 'This my brother Aleksi.'

Ted walked round to Aleksi's side and gave him the universally acknowledged signal to roll down his window. He couldn't have looked less like Desi if he tried. While Desi was bald, wiry and weasel-like, Aleksi was built like a brick outhouse.

'You must be Aleksi,' said Ted.

Aleksi shrugged and grunted something unintelligible, so Ted shouted across to Desi, 'Is he mute or something?'

228

'He talk only little English,' he replied.

Seemingly satisfied, Ted returned the clipboard to Desi. He was about to give Fergie the thumbs up when he paused, returned to Desi and asked, 'Can I see your passports?'

Desi rummaged through his pockets, pulled out two crumpled passports and handed them to Ted. It transpired that they were twins from Gabrovo in Bulgaria and their surname was Levkov. Ted scrutinised their photos then handed them back, saying, 'You don't look like twins to me.'

'That what everyone say,' laughed Desi.

Ted, who was beginning to feel more relaxed, finally gave Fergie the thumbs up and said to Desi, 'Can you ask Aleksi to give my mate a hand opening the gates while you turn the loader round and reverse it into the yard? It'll make it easier to load the cars.'

'No problem, boss,' replied Desi.

~~~

Starting with the desk, I swiftly moved from drawer to drawer. Apart from smutty magazines, a half-empty bottle of whisky and a well-squeezed tube of Anusol, there was no sign of the laptops. A quick look inside an old leather briefcase stashed beneath the desk was all I needed to complete the search.

Next were the filing cabinets. Starting at the bottom and working up, I methodically searched every drawer. But there was still no sign of the laptops so, turning my attention to the stationery cupboard, and using the same methodical method, it didn't take me long to ascertain they hadn't been hidden there. All that remained was the safe.

I just hope he's left it open.

I tried the handle but it wouldn't budge.

What to do now? I thought.

I tried the usual suspects: 0000, 1111, 1234, 4321 and 9876, but even Ted hadn't been stupid enough to use them. The fast approaching noise outside told me I'd run out of ideas and it was time to call it a day. Feeling deflated, I flopped onto Ted's chair and tried to figure out what to do next. That's when my eyes rested on the calendar. It had a picture of Ted standing in front of a clapped out banger waving a wad of banknotes. It read:

Blackstone Vehicle Recycling Centre

From Bone Shaker to Deal Breaker

For an instant quote call Ted Murphy on Warringsley 496 0779

Surely he's not been daft enough to use his phone number as the password. I keyed in the last four digits of the phone number and... voilà—the light on the keypad turned green. Tightly gripping the three-pronged handle, I continued turning until it came to a clunking stop. Then I pulled open the door.

With only the light from the workshop to guide me, I'd been able to systematically search the office, but the safe presented a new challenge. Positioned in the gloomiest part of the office, what scant light there had been, was completely obscured by the shadow of the open door. This made it almost impossible to see inside.

Having concentrated all my effort on my search, I'd failed to notice what had been under my nose all the time. It was only when I scanned the room for the light switch that I noticed the desk lamp. I was about to turn it on when I remembered the blinds were still open. Realising the lamp could act as a beacon to anyone entering the building, I ran to the window and peeped out. Seeing the workshop was deserted, I closed the blinds, returned to the desk, pointed the lamp towards the open safe, then flicked the switch.

With the exception of the bottom shelf, where three boxes had been neatly stacked, the shelves were laden with dusty files and well-worn folders. Suspecting something could be hidden behind them, I removed the boxes and set them down on the desk, then I lowered the arm of the anglepoise lamp and directed it into the void. To my relief, half hidden against the back wall, were three shiny laptops.

I could hear the transporter drawing closer and I knew, once it stopped its incessant noise, they'd be meeting up in the workshop.

To be certain they were our laptops, I picked out the one I thought was mine and held it under the lamp, then kept tilting it until the distinct outline of my Disney Princess stickers became visible. This confirmed these were indeed the stolen laptops.

Despite all that had happened, I'd managed to hang on to my trusty backpack. The original plan had been for Milly to help me carry the laptops. As it had been over an hour since I'd last seen her, I was hoping she'd managed to escape, find the twins then raise the alarm.

I took off my backpack, set it down on the desk, then tried to fit them all into the bag. But I soon discovered there was hardly room for one, let alone three! As it was Dad's computer we'd come for, I was left with no alternative but to leave the other two behind.

To ensure its safety, I took a fleece sweater from the backpack, wrapped it round the laptop, zipped up the bag, then slung it over my shoulder. Despite being packed and ready, the thought of leaving our laptops irked me. That's when I remembered the briefcase under Ted's desk. Having had the unpleasant task of inspecting it, I held it at arm's length and emptied its contents into the bin, then replaced them with our laptops.

All that remained was to return the boxes into the safe, tidy up the desk, then make my escape. I was about to place the final box into the safe when a thought crossed my mind. What could possibly be so valuable it has to be stored in metal boxes and locked in a safe? So I decided to investigate. To my surprise, when I opened the box, I found it filled with bundles of twenty-pound notes, each securely banded and labelled, '£1,000 in £20 NOTES'.

A quick look in the other boxes told me they were also full of cash.

Allowing my imagination to run away with me, I thought to myself, Imagine what I could do with all this money.'

Then a disapproving voice in my head, said, '*Rosemary Brown!*'

Yes, Sister Agnes?

Could you stand up and recite the eighth commandment, please?

Yes, Sister Agnes... thou shalt not steal.

Quite correct, Rosie. You may sit.

Nobody's going to notice if a couple of twenties go missing, I protested.

Rosemary!

Sorry, Sister Agnes.

Just my luck. As soon as I get my hands on some real money, Sister Agnes comes along and spoils it for me.

Begrudgingly returning the money to the safe, I gave one last rueful look, then slammed the door shut.

Why did I have to be brought up as a Catholic?

I switched off the lamp and hurried towards the window. Looking out, I could see the transporter's amber warning light reflecting off the whitewashed walls, indicating they'd almost arrived. I made my way to the door, locked it behind me, then tightened the straps on my backpack. With briefcase in one hand and keys in the other, I strode purposely down the corridor. When I reached the door, I slowly eased it open then peeped out. Once I was certain nobody was around, I stepped onto the landing and locked the door behind me, making sure I left the keys exactly where I'd found them. Then I made my way downstairs. I'd just reached the bottom when Ted entered. He was walking backwards, shouting and waving his arms in the air, trying to make himself heard above the ruckus.

Totally preoccupied, he'd failed to notice me standing at the foot of the stairs. Desperate for a place to hide, I dived under the nearest bench and watched, as outside, the lumbering juggernaut was slowly grinding to a halt.

'Get a move on,' yelled Ted, 'we need to get these little beauties loaded and off the premises ASAP. Oh and, by the way... Fergie, can you give Aleksi a hand with the ramps while I take Desi upstairs to sort out the paperwork?'

'Okay, Ted.'

'It's a bit gloomy in here, isn't it, Fergie? Ted asked. Why have you only turned on a couple of lights?'

'So as not to attract any unwanted attention. I thought it best to only turn on the ones nearest the doors,' replied Fergie.

'I think it's time we had them all on. We can't afford any slip-ups, especially tonight.'

'Okay, Ted, I'll do it now.'

A dozen fluorescent tubes flickered, flashed, then burst into life, flooding the workshop with a harsh, bright, all-encompassing light.

Fergie walked over to where Aleksi was busy performing his pre-loading checks. Tapping him on the shoulder, he said, 'While you're busy doing that, I'll drop ramps.'

Aleksi grabbed Fergie's arm, pointed to the workshop and grunted, 'Me know what do, you go wait.'

Suppressing his anger, he begrudgingly trudged to the workshop. After donning a fresh Tyvek suit, clean gloves and overshoes, he impatiently waited for Aleksi to give him the signal to start loading the cars.

Ted, closely followed by Desi, started climbing the stairs. Halfway up, Ted stopped, patted his pockets then called out, 'You've not seen my keys have you, Fergie?'

'You've not lost them again!' he exclaimed. 'The last time I saw you with them you were on your way to the office. Knowing you, you've probably left them hanging in the door.'

'Wouldn't surprise me,' replied Ted, 'I'd lose my head if it weren't screwed on.'

When they reached the top, Ted shouted back, 'You were right, Fergie, they're exactly where you said they'd be.'

With every light in the building switched on, I stood out like a sore thumb. It was only by sheer luck they hadn't seen me.

Making myself as inconspicuous as possible, I huddled under the bench and waited.

From my cramped position, I could see the white legs and blue overshoes of Fergie as he paced the floor, muttering foul oaths, all aimed at Aleksi, who was expertly making short work of the ramps.

'You start now,' shouted Aleksi.

Displaying the agility of a Formula One driver, Fergie leapt into one of the Ferrari's, switched on the engine and pressed down hard on the accelerator. Then, with spinning tyres, he screeched out of the garage. With my fingers firmly pressed in my ears, I braced myself for the inevitable, but instead of crashing, he performed an inch perfect handbrake turn, mounting ramps, rattling along the metal tracks, and with only centimetres to spare, he brought the car to an abrupt halt.

'What did you think of that?' he declared as he proudly climbed out of the driving seat.

'Glupako, pochti si razbil kolata!' roared Aleksi. (You fool, you almost crashed the car!)

Leaping off the trailer, he strutted towards the workshop shouting, 'That's easy for you buggers to say!'

To give him his due, for a complete moron, he was good at his job. In no time at all, he'd loaded both Ferraris, leaving Aleksi to secure them to the trailer.

Once fastened down, he covered them up. Then, operating the hydraulics, he hoisted them into the air, leaving the lower level available for the Porsche and the Maserati.

Although they were suspicious of each other, between the two of them they went about their business in a professional manner. It wouldn't be long before the trailer was fully loaded and ready to leave.

With Aleksi otherwise engaged, and Ted and Desi busy upstairs. If there was ever to be a perfect time to escape, this was it.

Without warning, Ted appeared at the top of the stairs, frantically gesticulating and shouting, 'Fergie, Fergie, come quick!'

'What's all the panic about, boss.'

'Someone's been in the safe!'

'I'm certain I saw you lock it.'

'You did. It must have happened while we were down at the gates.'

'Have they taken the loot?'

'That's what's odd about it; they didn't bother with the cash, they just took the laptops!'

'What kind of burglar breaks into a safe and doesn't take any money?'

'That's what I couldn't figure out... at first... then it dawned on me. What if the laptops were worth more than the cash?'

'What kind of laptops are worth more than forty grand? It's not as if they were gold plated or anything.'

'These days all the real money is stored digitally. It's obvious, whatever's on Brown's laptop is worth a hell of a lot more than forty grand. So the question is... who else knows about the laptop?'

'Brown, I suppose,' mused Fergie, 'but he's dead, so unless you're a clairvoyant, he's not in any position to tell us.'

'But what if someone else knows?' speculated Ted.

Fergie thought for a moment then exclaimed, 'They'd ignore the money and make straight for the laptops!'

'Well, done, Fergie. Now who would you say is the likeliest culprit?'

'The Brown girl!'

'Got it in one. So you know what that means, don't you?'

'I don't think I follow.'

'It means that if it was her, she might still be on the premises! Desi,' yelled Ted, 'get Aleksi to keep an eye on the door while we do a search of the building.'

I'd heard enough to know that if I didn't act quickly, they'd soon find me. Reluctantly leaving the briefcase behind, I broke cover and made for the door.

'There she goes,' roared Ted, 'grab her!'

In their haste, Ted and Desi fell over each other, collapsing in a tangled heap on the stairs. With Aleksi otherwise engaged, my only obstacle was Fergie. Having previously outwitted him, I felt confident of doing it again.

Feigning a dash to his right, I grabbed a nearby chair and hurled it at Fergie's legs.

Momentarily caught off balance, he made a valiant attempt to regain his footing and for one heart-stopping moment, I thought he'd succeeded. Then gravity took control. With the chair firmly entangled round his legs, the hapless hood went crashing to the floor.

Leaping over his flailing arms, I shot through the door and into the night. With young legs and a healthy lead, I was more than confident of making it to the gates before they had time to recover.

My dash for freedom was soon brought to a halt when a heavy hand gripped my collar, dragging me off my feet. Held in a vice-like grip, Aleksi carried me, kicking and screaming to where Ted and Desi were waiting.

'Well done, Aleksi,' said Ted, 'take her up to my office. I'll show her what happens to anybody who tries to cross me.'

Like Ann Darrow in King Kong's hand, no matter how much I spat, scratched and kicked, there was no way he was letting go.

When we reached Ted's office, he dropped me on the floor, grunting, 'You stop... boss come.'

As soon as Ted arrived, he ripped the bag from my back then, pointing, to a chair, he growled, 'Sit down and don't move.'

With eyes like saucers, I scanned the room, desperately looking for a means of escape. 'Don't even think about it,' said Ted. Then, opening a drawer, he pulled out some rope and a roll of gaffer tape. Handing them to Fergie, he ordered, 'Fasten her arms and legs and tie her to the chair.'

By the time he'd finished, I was trussed up like a ready-roast turkey.

Ted opened the backpack, removed Dad's laptop and powered it up. Then he said, 'If you know what's good for you, you'll give me the password.'

'Password... what password?'

'Don't play games with me. You know exactly what the password is. If you want to avoid any unpleasantness, be a good girl and give your Uncle Teddy the password.'

'I genuinely don't know the password. And even if I did, I wouldn't tell you!'

Ted leaned in, his tone unyielding. 'There are two ways we can handle this: the easy way or the hard way. So, which is it going to be?'

'Read my lips, I... DON'T... KNOW... THE... PASSWORD.'

Venting his anger on the desk, he gave it a sharp kick, sending it flying across the room. 'So you want to play hardball?' he growled.

He lurched towards me with a vengeful look on his face. Fearing the worst, I closed my eyes and waited. When nothing had happened, I opened my eyes and found him no longer there. A swift glance over my shoulder was enough to tell me all I needed to know.

Rheumatic fingers gripped my hair, dragging me back into the chair. To the accompaniment of squealing casters, he began swinging me round in stupefying circles. I was on the brink of fainting when he finally decided to relax his grip, sending me hurtling uncontrollably towards the desk. While still in a confused state, he grabbed my ear, gave it a violent twist, and said, 'This is just a sample of what to expect if you don't give me the password.'

I'd been full of bravado when I arrived, but now realised I was into something way beyond my control. Dazed, disoriented, scared, the tears began to flow.

'You can yell as much as you want, nobody's going to hear you.'

Pointing to Dad's laptop, Ted ordered, 'The password, NOW, and no funny business or I'll rearrange your pretty little face.'

In the forlorn hope something miraculous might happen, I tried stalling further. 'Why do you want to know what's in the laptop?' I blubbered.

'That's none of your business. Just keep your mouth shut and speak when you're spoken to.' Then he paused for a moment and said, 'I don't suppose it'll do any harm telling you. After all, you're not going be to be round long enough to tell anybody.'

Then he went into a rant.

'I'd been paying your dirty thieving, no good, rat of a dad a lot of money to manage my finances, but it seems he got greedy and decided to cream some off for himself. And I'm not talking peanuts. It's my money and I want it back!'

'My dad's not a thief,' I protested.

'We'll soon find out once you've given me the password.'

'That's going to be difficult.'

'Why's that?'

'Because I don't know it.'

'We spent weeks watching your house, hoping your mum would lead us to the money.'

'You didn't do a very good job of it, did you?' I sneered, 'I had you sussed long ago.'

'Shut your mouth or I'll shut it for you,' snarled Ted. 'Now where was I?'

'You were telling her we were watching her house,' reminded Fergie.

'Oh, yes, now I remember... after a while, I began to think she'd seen us and was pretending to be dippy just to throw us off the scent. Then it dawned on me, she actually was as dim as a Toc-H lamp, which meant, the only other person who could possibly lead us to the money was you. The night you came noseying around my car was just the opportunity we'd been waiting for. That's why we broke cover and tried to nab you.'

'And you didn't do a very good job of that, either.'

'What do you expect when you've got a sidekick like Fergie.

'Don't blame me, boss, I tried my best.'

'You didn't try hard enough, did you?'

'She's not like other girls, she's as slippery as an eel.'

'Luckily, it's turned out better than we could ever have expected.'

As he watched me squirming in the chair, Fergie grinned and said, 'You won't be giving us the slip anymore.'

Glorying in his success, Ted continued with his tale, 'The more I thought about it, the more certain I became that the info I wanted was stored on your dad's computer. That's why I half-inched the laptops. But there's only one thing puzzling me.'

'What's that?' I asked.

'How did you find us?'

'That was easy,' I lied, 'I spotted one of your calendars in the local chippy and recognised your face. I'd long suspected you of stealing the laptops but couldn't prove it. So, when I discovered where your hideout was, I decided to pay you an out-of-hours visit.'

'A right little Miss Marple, aren't you? You might think you're clever, but you have to be up bright and early to get one over on Ted Murphy. I'll give you five minutes to tell me the password. If you still won't tell me, you'll wish you'd never been born.'

I wanted to stay tight lipped but knew, one way or another, he'd eventually get the password out of me.

Looking nervously at his Rolex, Ted said, 'Okay, you've had long enough. Are you going to give me the password?'

'If you untie me, I'll log in for you.'

'What do you think, boss?' asked Fergie, 'can we trust her?'

'What harm can it do? She can't get very far with her legs tied together.'

As soon as Fergie untied my hands, I felt the blood returning to my fingers. To stall them further, I began to massage my hands and flex my fingers. Then, one exasperating joint after another, I started cracking my fingers, much to the annoyance of Ted, who said, angrily, 'Get on with it, we've not got all day.'

Desi, who'd been out of the room at the time, returned, saying, 'Aleksi's finished securing the cars so we're ready to go.'

'If you can hang on a little longer, I might have an extra piece of cargo for you.'

Not understanding the significance of this statement, I started to type in the password.

'Wait a second while I write it down,' ordered Ted.

Grabbing a notepad, he removed a Parker from his breast pocket then watched as I typed, O-P-E-N-S-E-S-A-M-E.

'Open bloody Sesame!' he exclaimed, 'how come I didn't think of that?'

'Cause you're stupid.'

'Don't push your luck little girl.'

Snatching the laptop from my hands, he quickly looked through Dad's files. By this time, Desi was getting impatient, reminding Ted, 'If we don't leave soon, we're going to miss the next tide.'

Slamming down the lid, Ted said, 'I've waited this long, so another few minutes isn't going to make any difference.'

'What's the extra cargo you were on about?' queried Desi.

'Good job you asked,' replied Ted, 'the captain's a friend of mine. He knows people in the Far East who'd pay a king's ransom for a blonde, twelve-year-old girl.'

'That's not fair,' protested Fergie, 'I should have first dibs. I've got mates who'd be very interested in her.'

'I've seen the scumbags you knock about with,' sneered Ted. 'They couldn't even afford one of her nail clippings.'

Still tied to the chair, I jumped to my feet, shouting, 'You bunch of perverts, you'll never get away with it.' Then I fell back onto the floor.

The peace was shattered by the shrill screech of metal-on-metal, closely followed by something heavy crashing to the ground.

'What the hell was that?' cried Ted.

'Sounds like one of the stacks has collapsed,' said Fergie.

'Go and check it out, Fergie,' ordered Ted.

Fergie raced down the stairs and out of the main door only to be greeted by the headlights of a fast approaching JCB. Behind the digger came the shrieks of a thousand banshees. Terrified, Fergie shot back up the stairs and ran into the office screaming, 'We've been rumbled, there's hundreds of the buggers out there and they're heading this way. It's every man for himself.'

Before Ted could calm the situation, Fergie had grabbed the car keys and was running as fast as his legs could carry him—out of the office, down the stairs and through the door. Before he had chance to reach the beamer, Paddy had wrestled him to the ground, twisting his arm up his back and forcing his face into the rough gravel.

'Okay, slime ball, what have you done with Rosie?'

'I can't breath,' he wheezed.

Just then, Billy Biggs arrived. 'If you've done anything to Rosie, I'll kill you.'

'I haven't touched her,' croaked Fergie,

Administering a sharp kick to the ribs, Billy barked, 'Just tell me where Rosie is.'

'Let me up and I'll tell you,' groaned Fergie.

Billy gave Paddy the nod and he released him.

'You nearly choked me,' he moaned.

'I'll strangle you with my bare hands if you don't tell me where Rosie is,' threatened Billy.

'She's upstairs in Ted's office,' croaked Fergie.

'How many more of you are there?' demanded Paddy.

'Only three,' gasped Fergie, 'they're with the girl.'

Paddy ordered two burly youths to guard Fergie, then shouted to the rest of the gang, 'Come on lads, let's get them.'

With an almighty roar, they grabbed whatever weapons were at hand and followed Paddy and Billy up the stairs. When they reached the corridor, Ted's office door was wide open. From where they were standing, they could see me tied to a chair with Ted's hand round my mouth.

'Stay back or the girl gets it,' ordered Ted.

Little did they know that the Levkov brothers, knives in hand, were stood on either side of the door. While Ted was temporarily distracted, I took my chance and sank my teeth into the skin between his finger and thumb. Screaming in agony, he released his grip.

'Watch out,' I shouted, 'they're hiding behind the door!'

Having lost the element of surprise, the Levkov brothers came out to face the ever-growing crowd.

'Put those knives down before somebody gets hurt,' demanded Paddy.

Realising the game was up, they threw their weapons to the floor.

Ted, holding his bloodied hand, screamed, 'You spineless halfwits, you could at least have put up a fight.'

Looking past Paddy, I could see Milly and the twins anxiously waiting. With the stand-off over, they pushed past Paddy and ran towards me.

'You look awful,' said Milly, 'what have they done to you?'

'Apart from a few bumps and grazes, I think I'll survive.'

They dragged Fergie in and forced him to sit on the floor with the rest of the gang, then waited for the police to arrive.

When Ted heard the rapidly approaching squad cars, a look of abject panic flashed across his face. Looking pleadingly at Paddy, he said, 'Are you sure you want the police sniffing round the place? Once they've finished with us, they'll probably end up searching your place as well. I'm sure you've got nothing to hide, but you know what they're like, once they start poking their noses into your business, who knows what they're going to find.'

Billy's eyes widened, 'He's got a point, Paddy.'

Seeing Paddy wavering, Ted decided to up the ante.

'See that safe over there,' gestured Ted, 'if you look inside, you'll find three metal boxes on the bottom shelf. When you open them, you'll find forty-thousand smackers in used notes. It's all yours if you let us go.'

Billy whispered to Paddy, 'What he's saying makes a lot of sense, Pat. Why should we help the police? They've never done anything for us—and think what we could do with all that money.'

Then Beryl and Brenda decided to intervene. 'Dad! How could you? Don't forget why we came here. Milly put her trust in us so we can't let her down now. You only have to look at the state of

Rosie to know what might have happened if we hadn't have arrived when we did.'

With the look of someone who'd lost a pound and found a penny, Billy said, 'The girls are right, Paddy. Anybody who can do something like that to a twelve-year-old girl deserves all that's coming to them.'

Realising the ordeal was finally over, I started to cry like a baby. Milly, throwing out her arms, gave me a big hug. 'Yeow,' I yelped, 'not so hard!'

'Sorry, Rosie. I don't know my own strength.'

She passed me a tissue and waited until I'd composed myself. Then, in a tearful voice, I said, 'I can't tell you how relieved I am to see you.' Attempting a feeble joke, I continued, 'If you'd left it any longer, I'd have probably ended up in the back streets of Bangkok.'

'Bangkok!' exclaimed Milly, 'what on earth are you talking about?'

'Never mind. I'll tell you later.' Then, trying not to be overheard, I whispered something in her ear.

'You'll have to speak up,' said Milly, 'with all the kerfuffle, I can't hear a word you're saying.'

Leaning closer, I muttered, 'I've only gone and wet myself!'

CHAPTER EIGHTEEN

Paddy and Billy instructed a couple of his lads to keep guard while they went out to meet the police. Over the years, the gypsies had had numerous run-ins with the police, often relating to stolen scrap metal or somebody trespassing on Sir Hugo Davenham's estate, so it was understandable that they were reluctant to engage with them. But for the girl's sake, Billy was prepared to swallow his pride and help them. Meanwhile, Milly, concerned about my appearance and dignity, suggested to the twins, 'Why don't we take Rosie to the toilets and freshen her up before the police arrive? You don't mind, do you, Rosie?'

Feeling like I'd fallen into a cesspit, I readily agreed. Despite their best efforts, with only a wash basin, hand dryer and Swarfega at our disposal, it was abundantly clear it would never be sufficient.

'It's no use,' sighed Brenda, 'we're going to have to take you back to our place and ask Mum to fix you up. Once you're presentable, we can come back and clarify everything with the police.

Smelling like a sewer rat, I readily agreed.

'Best hurry,' said Milly, 'the police will be here soon and they're bound to want to speak to us.'

As I made the uncomfortable walk to the gypsy camp, behind us sirens wailed and blue lights flashed. 'We should have at least waited until the police arrived,' I protested.

'Do you really want to spend the rest of the evening sitting in soggy undies while talking to the police?' asked Beryl. 'You'd probably end up catching the dreaded lurgy... or worse!'

I was about to ask her what could possibly be worse than the dreaded lurgy but I decided it was better off not knowing.

'Another half hour isn't going to do any harm,' said Beryl, reassuringly, 'I'm sure Dad and Uncle Paddy are more than capable of holding the fort till we get back. Once Mum's sorted you out with a shower and some clean clothes, you'll feel like a million dollars.'

They were right, of course, but knowing Ted like I did, I couldn't relax until they were safely under lock and key. Ted's as slippery as an eel at the best of times, but back him into a corner and who knows what he could do. I had an uneasy feeling he still had a trick or two up his sleeve.

~~~

'I'm Inspector Russell' said the officer, speaking to nobody in particular, 'and this is Sergeant Griffiths. My men are currently in the process of clearing the premises and cordoning off the area. Now, could somebody tell me what's been happening here?'

Ted, seizing his chance, said, 'Am I glad to see you, inspector, I'm Edward Murphy, owner and proprietor of this establishment. And these brave fellows (pointing to Fergie and the Levkov's) are my trusted employees, so I can personally vouch for their integrity.'

Paddy attempted to interrupt, but the inspector cut him short, saying, 'You can have your say once I've heard Mr Murphy's version of events!'

'This is just a formality, Mr Murphy, but I'm obliged to ask if you could you show me some identification.'

'Certainly, inspector!' Pulling a bulging wallet from his pocket, he produced his driver's licence.

To add to his credibility, he pointed to a framed document on the wall and said, 'And that's my operating certificate.'

The inspector handed back the driver's licence then walked over to examine the certificate. Looking suitably impressed, he said, 'Everything seems in order, Mr Murphy. Now, in your own words, tell me exactly what happened.'

'What happened?' exploded Paddy, 'what do you mean, what happened, it's me you should be asking. Not him!'

'Keep your mouth shut, and don't open it again until I tell you!'

'We run a twenty-four hour business and I was preparing a late night delivery,' said an increasingly confident Ted, 'when there was a huge bang. At first I thought it was another of them there earthquakes we keep getting from all the frackin' that's going on down the road, then a huge JCB came roaring down the track towards us, followed by this pack of bogtrotters.'

'We tried to defend ourselves but were soon outnumbered. They must have found out where I keep the takings cos this fella,' pointing to Paddy, 'frogmarched me up the stairs carrying a machete, then threatened to cut off my ears if I didn't open the safe. If you lot hadn't turned up when you did, I'd have ended up like that Van Gough bloke. I don't know who it was who called you, but I'm certainly glad they did.'

'It's a pack of lies,' protested Billy. 'My daughter's friend, Rosie, was being held hostage by these... these... whatever they are, and we came here to rescue her.'

'And where's this mysterious friend now?' asked the inspector.

'They've taken her to the toilets to clean her up. After they'd finished with her, she was in a right mess.'

'Sergeant!'

'Yes, sir!'

'Nip down and see if you can find them.'

'Right away, sir.'

He soon returned, saying, 'Nobody down there, inspector.'

'There must be,' exclaimed Billy, 'are you sure you've had a proper look?'

'Yes,' said the sergeant. Then, looking closely at Paddy, he said, 'Weren't you the one I nicked for poaching pheasants on Sir Hugo's estate?'

'What's that got to do with anything?' said Paddy.

'I thought so,' said Griffiths, 'I never forget a face!'

'That does it,' said the inspector, 'you're under arrest.'

'Arrest?' protested Paddy, 'for what?'

'For assault, attempted robbery and criminal damage. And that's just for starters. Read them their rights, Griffiths.'

'I am arresting you under suspicion of armed robbery,' quoted Griffiths, 'You do not have to say anything, but...'

'You're making a big mistake,' shouted Paddy, 'they're the criminals, not us.'

'Criminality's a way of life for you lot,' said the inspector, dismissively.

'You're letting them get off scot-free!' exclaimed Billy.

'The way I see it,' proclaimed the inspector, 'is that Mr Murphy and his men were going about their lawful business when you broke in, attacked them, threatened them with violence, then tried to steal their takings. With your record, you could be looking at a long stretch.'

'You were right, Billy,' said Paddy, 'never trust a copper.'

'Cuff 'em and run 'em down to the station, sergeant.'

254

'Right away, inspector!'

'Good job we arrived when we did, Mr Murphy,' said the inspector, 'God knows what they might have done to you. All we need now is to round up the rest of the gang, then we can leave you in peace to get on with your work. Oh, and by the way, you've got some lovely cars on that transporter. They must have cost you a fortune.'

'It's just a sideline at the moment,' replied Ted, 'but if it all works out, I hope to move out of the scrap business and open my own dealership. Will you be requiring a statement, inspector?'

Checking the time, he said, 'It's getting late and I can see you've got a lot of work to do, so I won't detain you any longer. I'll send a man round in the morning to interview you.'

'Thank you, inspector. I don't know what we'd have done without you.'

'All part of the service, Mr Murphy, just doing my job.'

'And it's a fine job you're doing,' replied Ted in a phoney Irish accent.

'We don't just spend our time trying to catch speeding motorists like some people think,' boasted the inspector, 'we're also out catching real villains like these!'

Once they were safely out of sight, Ted heaved a sigh of relief, saying, 'Where the hell did they get that inspector from? If brains were dynamite, he wouldn't have enough to blow his nose.'

'What do we do now, Ted,' asked Fergie, nervously, 'they're bound to cotton on to us—eventually?'

'We stick to the plan. Desi, Aleksi—get those motors down to the docks ASAP and make sure they're loaded onto the ship. Once you're done, you can dump the transporter and disappear, preferably back to Bulgaria.'

'What are we going to do?' asked Fergie.

'That copper might be as thick as a brick but even he's going to suss us out eventually. But by the time he does, we'll be miles away from here. Come on, Fergie, no time to waste. Let's take everything that can implicate us, load it all into the beamer, then we can disappear into the night, preferably somewhere up north where we can lie low until the heat's off.'

~~~

Mrs Biggs stripped me down to my birthday suit then wrapped a housecoat round me while she ran the shower. Looking round, I was surprised at just how much room there was in these caravans.

'I've thrown your clothes in the wash,' shouted Mrs Biggs, 'once you're dry, I'll put some of the girls' clothes out on the chair for you. They might not be quite your size, but they're clean and dry and it's the best I can do under the circumstances.'

'That's okay, Mrs Biggs,' I shouted, 'sorry for the mess, anything's better than what I was wearing.'

I came out of the shower room wearing ill-fitting undies and a baggy, grey tracksuit.

'Very fetching,' skitted Milly, 'you look as if you've just stepped off the front cover of Vogue Magazine!'

Frowning, Mrs Biggs said, 'Ignore her, Rosie, they'll do till you get home.'

Once I'd put on my shoes and socks, I said, 'I really think we need to get back to the scrapyard and tell the police what happened.'

'You're not going out again,' ordered Mrs Biggs, 'you'll catch your death.'

'But what about the police?'

'Leave that to Billy and Paddy, they'll sort it all out.'

Just then I heard the familiar sound of an approaching car.

'I wonder who that could be.' said Mrs Biggs.

'If my ears aren't deceiving me,' I answered, 'I'd say it was Mum!'

Mrs Biggs ran out and flagged her down, 'If you're looking for Rosie and Milly, they're in here with me.'

Mum slammed on the brakes and almost hit the caravan as she skidded to a halt. Throwing open the door, she ran to the caravan and, completely ignoring Mrs Biggs, shouted, 'Where is she?'

'It's alright, Mum,' I called out, 'I'm quite safe.'

'Is Milly with you?' she demanded, 'her mum's going frantic!'

'Here I am, Mrs Brown,' shouted Milly.

'Come on, Milly. Grab your stuff and let's get you home.' Then, turning to me, she said, 'And as for you, young lady, you've got a lot of explaining to do!'

Mrs Biggs stepped forward and said, 'Don't be too hard on them, Mrs Brown, they deserve a medal for what they've done.'

Mum, completely blanking her out, shouted, 'Come on you two, jump in the car and let's get you out of this hellhole.'

'Once I've washed and ironed Rosie's clothes,' shouted Mrs Biggs, 'I'll get Billy to bring them round to your house!'

'I wouldn't bother,' she mumbled, 'I'll only have to wash and disinfect them.'

Mum didn't even look sideways as she sped away from the camp. 'Mum,' I pleaded, 'we really need to go to the scrapyard to let Mr Biggs know we're both okay.'

'I'm sure Mr Biggs and his mates are more than capable of managing without you,' sneered Mum, 'so just sit quietly in the back until you get home.'

If I'd have had the slightest inkling as to what was happening to Paddy and Billy, I'd have created such a fuss, Mum would have had no alternative but to drive me to the police station to tell them the truth about Ted and Fergie. Then they'd have been able to arrest them before they made good their escape—but how was I to know?

Once she'd dropped Milly off, Mum maintained the silent treatment until we got home. Once inside, she said, 'Get those manky clothes off while I run you a bath; then it's straight to bed for you, m'lady.'

I did my best to protest but she was in no mood to listen. I'd have to wait until the morning when, hopefully, she'd finally calmed down, then I'd be able to explain everything.

~~~

Early next morning, there came a knock on the door. I listened as Mum clopped down the stairs to the door. 'Inspector Maitland!' she exclaimed, 'what a pleasant surprise! Won't you come in.'

Doffing his cap, he said, 'I'm afraid this isn't a social visit, Mrs Brown. I'm here on official business. I've brought WPC Becky Williams along with me to take witness statements. I've been informed an incident occurred yesterday evening at a vehicle recycling centre on Blackstone Lane and young Rosie was involved. Could we speak to her, please?'

'Certainly,' said Mum, 'she's not up yet; I'll just pop up to her room and see if she's awake.'

'If you wouldn't mind, Mrs Brown, it's extremely urgent.'

I'd already put on my dressing gown and slippers and was sat on the bed with my back to her when she entered.

'Inspector Maitland's here and he'd like to speak to you,' Mum said. 'It must be very important because he's brought a policewoman with him, so don't keep them waiting!'

'Okay, Mum, I'll be straight down.'

As I entered the lounge, Mum, WPC Williams and Inspector Maitland were sat patiently waiting for me to arrive. When she saw me, Mum gasped in horror, 'What on earth's happened to your face?'

I ran to the mirror and saw a face I barely recognised staring back at me. It had two black eyes and a swollen face.

'I think it's time you explained yourself,' said the inspector, 'and this time I want the truth.'

I told him where I'd first encountered Ted and Fergie, about the burglary and the search for the missing laptops, how Ted had managed to catch me, how he'd roughed me up for the password, how he'd planned to abduct and sell me into child slavery, and crucially, how Paddy and the gang had come to my rescue.

'That bloody dipstick, Russell,' he said, 'he's only gone and arrested the wrong people. No wonder the Met got rid of him. Apparently, he was so inept they had to push him out, and we ended up with him.'

'I'll get on the blower straight away and send a couple of squad cars round to the scrapyard to pick them up,' said WPC Williams.

'Thanks, Becky, but if I was Murphy, or whatever his name is, I'd be long gone. As soon as the Super finds out what's happened, Russell and Griffiths are in for the biggest rollicking they've ever had.'

'But what about my rescuers?' I asked.

'I'll have them released immediately. They'll probably threaten to sue us for wrongful arrest and unlawful imprisonment—and to be honest, who could blame them?'

'Did you manage to get all that, Becky?'

'Yes, inspector,' she replied.

If the rollicking those two incompetents were about to receive was just a fraction of the one Mum gave me, then I felt sorry for them. '...and don't think I'm going to forget what you did!' she ended.

Later that day, Nigel Maitland returned. This time he was on his own. Mum, who couldn't disguise her admiration, said, 'Make yourself comfortable, inspector, while I make you a nice cup of tea.'

'I'm sorry to tell you, but as I surmised, they'd already gone by the time my men arrived. They took everything with them.'

'Did you find our laptops?' I asked.

'I looked where Rosie told me, but there was no sign of them. They could be anywhere by now.'

'If they've still got the laptops, then why don't you use the tracker to find them?' I suggested.

'Surely they wouldn't be stupid enough to leave the laptops switched on,' he muttered. Then he said, 'It's a long shot, but it just might work. Can I take Rosie down to the station with me so she can log into our computers to see if we can trace the laptops?'

'I'll take her,' said Mum, 'you drive on ahead and we'll follow.'

'I'll just ring the station to let them know we're coming,' he replied.

They'd already set up the computer when we arrived, so I sat down and logged into the tracker. A map of the Lancashire coast appeared with a map pin, pointing to a location somewhere in Westhaven on Sea.

'Can we zoom in closer?' asked the inspector.

'I'll see what I can do,' said the constable.

He managed to narrow the map to within a half mile then said, 'This is the best I can do.'

Out of the numerous hotels and boarding houses lining the seafront, the map pin was pointing to The Imperial Hotel. 'Quick Constable, get on the blower to the lads in Lancashire and ask them to send a couple of squad cars to The Imperial Hotel in Westhaven on Sea straight away.' Then, turning to us, he said, 'They've probably spent most of the night driving so with a bit of luck they should still be tucked up in bed. They'll get the shock of their lives when they wake up to find our lads waiting outside the bedroom door.'

We returned home and even though she'd had more than enough time to get over it, there was still an uneasy atmosphere in the house. So I decided it best if I kept out of her way. I crept upstairs to my room and lay on the bed, but soon became bored. I know what I'll do, I thought, I think I'll read a book... but what shall I read? I know, I'll start reading the book Aunt Tracy bought me last Christmas. So I tiptoed to the bookshelf and pulled out "Love Frankie by Jaqueline Wilson".

Making myself comfortable, I opened the book and started to read...

'I haven't got a clue what I'm going to give anyone for Christmas,' I said, sighing.

'Me neither,' said Sam.

The more I read, the heavier my eyelids became. Suddenly, I was awakened by the sound of the telephone ringing downstairs. I sneaked to the door and listened.

'Brown residence...

Oh, it's you, Nigel, how lovely to...

You've caught them!...

They're at the station now!...

She's asleep at the moment...

Urgent!...

I'll wake her...

See you in ten...

Byee!'

I ran to my bed and lay with the book in my hand pretending to be asleep.

'Rosie, wake up. Great news... they finally managed to catch two of the men. They've been arrested and are being held in Warringsley Police Station. The inspector wants you to go down to identify them!'

When we got there, Nigel was standing at the entrance wearing a plastic smile as he waited patiently to greet us. 'Those can't be his own teeth,' I commented, 'they're far too white and shiny.'

'You'll end up with false teeth if you don't look after them,' replied Mum, curtly.

As we followed him into the station, we passed Russell and Griffiths glumly sitting at their desks. To rub salt in their wounds, the inspector bellowed, 'We've already given your friends a fully apology, Rosie, then we escorted them home.'

When we arrived at the interrogation suites, they'd put Fergie in one room and Ted in another. 'Can you look through this window and tell me if this is the man who assaulted you?' asked Nigel. 'Take your time, there's no hurry, and don't worry, they can't see you... it's one-way glass.'

Ted was sat, head in his hands, waiting to be interrogated. 'That's him,' I said, 'that's Ted.' He took me to the next window then asked, 'What about him?'

'Yes, he's the one they call Fergie.'

'Thank you, Rosie, you've been a great help. Now if you'll follow me to the office, I've prepared a statement for you to sign. Read it carefully and once you're happy, you can sign it. Then you're free to return home.'

'Is that it?' I asked.

With a smile of satisfaction, he said, 'For the time being.'

Following their interrogation, Ted and Fergie were taken to the cells to be held overnight.

Before he left, Nigel Maitland decided to pay them a final visit.

'Well, lads, bit of a change from The , isn't it?'

'What I can't understand,' lamented Ted, 'is how you managed to find us so quickly.'

'That was easy,' said the inspector, 'you forgot to turn the laptop off so we were able to track your movements.'

'What did I tell you about that bloody laptop?' Fergie shouted from the adjoining cell, 'you should have lashed it in the crusher when you had the chance!'

For the first time ever, Ted was lost for words.

Once the inspector saw them safely locked up for the night, he shouted, 'Goodnight lads. Make sure you get a good night's sleep because you'll be up bright and early in the morning and on your way to HMP Woodford!'

CHAPTER NINETEEN

I arrived home to find a shiny black limousine sitting outside our house. Throwing open the door, I shouted, 'I'm home, Mum!'

'Quick! Come into the living room,' she shouted, 'there's somebody here to see you.'

Wondering who my unexpected guest could be, and dropping everything, I ran into the lounge. Sitting opposite Mum, looking resplendent in a smart new uniform, was Inspector Nigel Maitland.

Unable to disguise my disappointment, I muttered, 'If it isn't Inspector Maitland... and here I was thinking we'd had a visit from the lord mayor.'

'It's Chief Inspector Maitland now,' said Mum, proudly. 'Hasn't he done well?'

'If you call arresting the wrong people and letting the real villains escape, then yes, he's done very well indeed.'

'You know full well it wasn't Nigel's fault!' protested Mum.

He fixed me with a cold, hard stare, then said, 'Sit down, Rosie. I've got some questions to ask you.'

Slouching on the couch, I sighed, 'What do you want to know?'

'Just a couple of minor points to clear up, then I'll be on my way.'

'You sound just like Columbo,' I joked. 'Okay, lieutenant, fire away!'

'When I came round to investigate the stolen laptops, I asked if you knew your dad's password, and you said you didn't. That was a lie, wasn't it?'

'No!' I replied.

'I think you were deliberately trying to obstruct me in my investigations.'

'It wasn't like that!' I stuttered.

'Give me one good reason why I shouldn't charge you with withholding information?'

'I admit, I might have told a little white lie.'

'Black or white, they're still lies. I think it's time you told me the truth.'

Taking a deep breath, I said, 'Okay, I'll tell you everything... at the time, I had no idea what the password was. I only discovered it much later.'

'Carry on, Rosie, I'm all ears.'

'So I see!'

'Less of the levity, young lady, you're already skating on thin ice as it is.'

Clearing my throat, I continued, 'When the constable returned Dad's briefcase, it was in such a bad state, Mum told me to get rid of it. For some strange reason, I had a feeling there was something inside the case Dad wanted me to see so I removed the contents and dumped the briefcase in the dustbin. Then when Mum wasn't looking, I took the documents up to my room and hid them in my wardrobe.'

'Once you'd hidden the documents, what did you do then?'

'I waited till Mum had settled down in front of the telly for the night. Then, using the excuse of working on a school project, I returned to my room and started wading through his papers. It was getting late and I was about to call it a day when a letter addressed to 'Miss Rosebud' caught my eye. As Dad often called me 'Little Miss Rosebud', I knew he'd written it for me.'

'So what was in the letter?'

'I couldn't make head nor tail of it. It was just financial stuff.'

'So what made you think it contained a hidden message?'

'He wouldn't have written it if there wasn't one.'

'True.'

'It took me a while to solve the riddle, but when I did, I got so carried away with my success that I decided to try and find the laptops myself using the tracker.'

'That's another thing you lied about,' interrupted the inspector. 'I specifically asked you if there were any trackers on the laptops and you said there wasn't.'

'You might have asked Mum, but you certainly didn't ask me.'

'You must have realised I was referring to the pair of you when I asked the question, yet you didn't say a thing. Anyway, I digress—please continue.'

'In short, when I saw the map pin was pointing towards the gypsy camp, I naturally assumed one of the gypsies had taken our laptops.'

'So you naturally assumed the gypsies were thieves, eh? And you accuse the police of being prejudiced.'

'To my shame... yes, I did.'

'It's a good job your gypsy friends can't hear you now. They'd never speak to you again. Once again, I digress, please continue with your story.'

'As the gypsies know us, I decided to pay our friends—the twins—a visit and asked Milly to come along with me. The plan was, while we were playing games with the twins, Milly would distract them and I'd sneak off to try and find the laptops.'

'As we were approaching the camp, we decided to check the tracker again, just to see if we could pinpoint their exact location. That's when we found out they weren't in the camp at all, but in the scrapyard next door.'

'Once you knew that, why didn't you call the police?'

'Since the place looked to be deserted, and we were already outside, we decided we'd have a quick look around to see if we could find out where they'd hidden them. It was just our luck that the gang happened to turn up when they did, otherwise our plan would have worked. But by then it was too late.'

'That still doesn't justify your actions,' reproached Nigel. 'It's lucky for you the police arrived when they did.'

'I know I messed up, and I'm really sorry about it, but I honestly believed we had a good chance of finding them.'

'So you thought you could do a better job than the police, eh?'

'Not exactly better, just... well... differently.'

Bending down, he opened his briefcase and removed a framed certificate. Adopting an official tone, he declared, 'In recognition of your role in the capture and arrest of the car thieves, the chief constable has asked me to present you with this Certificate of Commendation.'

I reluctantly accepted the award then discreetly slipped it down the side of the couch.

There was an uneasy silence before Mum said, 'What do you have to say, Rosie?'

'Thank you,' I mumbled.

'You've earned it, Rosie,' Inspector Maitland replied.

Rapidly changing the subject, he said, 'You're probably wondering why Murphy and Ferguson were watching your house.'

'To be honest, I didn't know who they were, but I had a feeling it was something to do with Dad's business dealings. It was only later I realised just how desperate they were.'

'Once we had them in custody, Ferguson started to sing like a canary. From what he told us, we were able to piece it all together. Over the past few years, an unusually large number of high-end sports cars were being reported stolen and never recovered. These apparently unrelated events led Scotland Yard to conclude that an organised gang of car thieves was responsible.'

'Following enquiries, they had a tip-off that the gang was operating in our area. But with little to go on, we were at a loss to discover where. Our big break came when the stock market crashed and gang leader, Ted Murphy, ordered an audit of his accounts, revealing a substantial amount of money had gone missing.'

'Realising the only possible culprit was Mr Brown, Murphy and Ferguson decided to put the squeeze on him. Unfortunately, his subsequent disappearance and tragic loss soon put paid to their plans. Convinced he must have a secret bank account, they concluded that one of you must know of its location.'

'After many wasted hours watching your house, it dawned on them that the information they were seeking was probably stored on Mr Brown's laptop, so they decided to break into your house and steal it. So to make it look like an opportunist

271

robbery, they stole all three laptops. Little did they know, that your laptop had a tracker on it.'

Turning to me, he said, 'In your determination to find the laptops, you inadvertently stumbled upon their hideout, but instead of doing the sensible thing, you ended up putting both you and your friend's lives in danger. Instead of presenting you with an award, I ought to be dragging you over the coals for what you did, but reluctantly, I have to concede that without your bravery and perseverance, we might never have cracked this case.'

'Milly and the lads from the gypsy camp are the real heroes, not me,' I replied.

'Be that as it may,' he said, 'once we'd gained access to Mr Brown's personal files, we were able to hand them over to our financial crimes investigation team. Between you, me and the lamp post, I've been told they're encountering substantial difficulties trying to unravel the intricate web of financial products and offshore accounts he'd set up.'

'What about Desi and Aleksi?' I asked.

'We've still not caught them, but it shouldn't be long. We're watching all the ports and airports, and as soon as they attempt to leave the country we'll have them.'

'But they were driving a bloody great car transporter with four cars on it,' I said, angrily, 'you can't easily hide something like that!'

'How many times have I told you about using bad language in the house?' berated Mum, 'it's those schoolmates of yours, they're as common as muck. Sorry, Nigel, you were saying...'

'Like I said, we're still looking for them.'

'You mentioned something about compensation,' asked Mum, hopefully. 'Does that include us?'

'We're well aware of your financial situation, Mavis, but unfortunately you're at the wrong end of a very long line of victims.'

'So what you're telling me is, once the vultures have picked clean the carcass, we can have what's left.'

'Sadly, Mavis, that appears to be the case.'

'So let me get this straight. I lose my beautiful home, end up destitute, our house is looted, my daughter's held hostage and brutally beaten, and all we get to show for it are a few measly bones to pick over. If that's the thanks you get for being decent, honest citizens, then they can stick their compensation right up their jacksies!'

Nigel put his arm round Mum's shoulder and said, 'I know it's cruel, Mavis, but unfortunately that appears to be the legal position.'

Placing a hand on his heart, he said, 'Mark my words, Mavis, as long as my name's Nigel Walter Maitland, I promise I'll move heaven and earth to ensure you receive the best possible compensation.'

Walter! So he is a Wally after all!

'Thank you, Nigel,' said Mum, 'I realise it's not your fault, sorry I got so angry.'

'There's no need to apologise, Mavis, your anger is quite understandable.'

'It's just the injustice of it all,' sobbed Mum.

~~~

Autumn gave way to winter and to make matters worse, Mum injured her back when she foolishly tried to lift Mrs Begley off the floor and into a chair. Since then, she'd been unable to work for weeks. With Christmas just around the corner, things were looking grim.

We'd all but given up on compensation when a knock came to the door. 'I hope it's not that window cleaner after his Christmas tip,' muttered Mum as she walked to the door.

'If it isn't Chief Inspector Maitland. To what do we owe the pleasure?' she quipped. 'Don't tell me. Our home has just been repossessed, and you've brought the bailiffs round to kick us out!'

Ignoring her cutting remark, he announced, 'I've come to let you know that all of the money has been recovered and is to be distributed between the major creditors. Once they've all been paid, your share will come out of whatever remains.'

'Go on,' sneered Mum, 'make my day; tell me how much money I owe them.'

Disregarding her cynicism, Nigel explained, 'It appears your husband was something of a financial genius. He established a series of intricate investment vehicles and offshore accounts, investing eighty per cent of the gang's funds while retaining twenty per cent for himself. By ensuring the money was constantly in motion, detection was extremely difficult. After being sent down numerous rabbit holes and blind alleys, our team eventually traced the cash to an account in the Cayman Islands.'

'Cayman Islands,' gasped Mum, 'why there?'

'It's used as an offshore tax haven by the rich and famous to hide their wealth.'

Intrigued, Mum asked, 'So how much did he have in this account?'

'It's hard to say at the moment, he'd converted it all into Bitcoins.'

'Bitcoins! What on earth are they?'

'Good question, and one I also asked. According to our tech team, it's a type of cryptocurrency.'

'I'm still none the wiser.'

'It's a form of electronic currency. They were something of a novelty at the time and not many people were aware of them, but your husband must have spotted their potential and took a gamble. And from what we've seen so far, it seems to have paid off handsomely.'

'How much did he pay for them?' asked Mum.

'When he first bought them, they cost him £50,000.'

'Fifty thousand?' she gasped, 'so what are they worth now?'

'Give or take a couple of grand, we estimate them to be valued at approximately ... fifteen million.'

'Fifteen million pounds!' cried Mum, 'you've got to be joking!'

'Yes, fifteen million pounds,' he replied, 'and that's based on current estimates. The way these things are increasing in value, they could be worth double that by the time everything's sorted.'

Momentarily lost for words, Mum jumped to her feet, let out an ear-piercing shriek, threw her arms round me, and screamed, 'We're rich, we're bloody rich.' Then, lifting me off my feet, she whirled me round and round the room singing, 'We're in the money, we're in the money, dee doodle-doodle-doodle-doodle-dee do.'

Chief Inspector Maitland patiently sat watching us dance around the room. Then he stood up, clapped loudly and shouted, 'Ladies! Please! Could you sit down a minute while I explain things?'

Stepping off cloud nine, we flopped, exhausted, into our chairs.

'Okay, ladies. Have either of you heard of The Proceeds of Crime Act?'

We both shook our heads.

'I didn't think you had,' he said. 'To put it simply, the police have the power to confiscate all monies or assets obtained by criminals in the course of their activities. Unfortunately, this also includes fraud and money laundering which, in your husband's situation, appears to have been the case. The Assets

Recovery Agency is currently collating his assets. Once their work is over, it's down to the courts to decide how the money is to be allocated.'

Sensing our disappointment, he tried cheering us up by saying, 'I don't want to build up your hopes but I believe, as a victim of his fraudulent activities, you may be entitled to a share of the money.'

~~~

When all of the money was finally recovered, it was estimated that Dad had amassed assets of more than £21.3 million. Mum, with the help of Nigel, immediately made an application for compensation and, following much deliberation, the judge awarded her... wait for it... £7.5 million!

Finally, Mum could give up her job, start searching for her dream home in the country, then resume the life she'd previously enjoyed. But was that what I wanted?

Over the past few months, I'd had many adventures—some good, some bad—making new friends along the way. Did I really want to turn my back on all this? And most of all... what about my best friend, Milly?

THE END